HOSPITAL NURSE

Lucy Agnes Hancock

WILDSIDE PRESS

CHAPTER ONE

THE EARLY TWILIGHT OF A rainy October day was casting shadows in the room. Irene Barker and Kathy Marshall stood before a window in the nurses' annex watching the traffic as it slid down the long hill on which Bostwick Memorial Hospital spread its great bulk like a protecting mother hen over the city in the valley below.

"There goes the ambulance again, Barker," the younger nurse murmured, as the big gray car sped down the drive and out into traffic. The siren shattered the almost brooding quiet, and in a moment the car was out of sight as the two nurses mused aloud as to its possible destination.

"You're welcome to Receiving, Marshall," Barker told her, shrugging plump shoulders. "That's one job I hate."

"But why? Now, I rather like it," the other countered. "Certainly one is never bored there, while private duty, especially at night, is far from interesting."

"Oh, all private cases aren't like old lady Bates, Kathy," the older nurse pointed out. "I sometimes wonder why such people come to a hospital. Too much money, maybe, or it might be the desire for attention."

"Could be," Kathy answered, "and in her case I have an idea it was attention she wanted. By the way, hasn't she any family—grandchilden, nieces, or nephews? She had no callers while I was on duty."

"Oh, yes, she has scads of relatives, but she seems to dislike them all—won't have any of them around her. Merriman told me she gave strict orders that not one was to be admitted to her room. Was she hard to take care of?"

Kathy Marshall shook her head. "On the contrary, she was too easy. I really had nothing to do. She just lay and slept all night, quietly. She asked for nothing. She ate what was brought to her, required practically no medications, and talked very little. I found it extremely trying. It was a relief to me when she decided to go south for the winter. Dr. Elliott told me that she is immensely wealthy, but that she doesn't seem to take any pleasure in her money. I wish I had some of it. It must be wonderful to have all the money one wants, for a while at least."

"Money isn't so much, Kathy," the older nurse answered. "It isn't money that insures happiness. There isn't money

3

enough in the world to buy health, for instance, or love—or what passes for love."

Kathy Marshall laughed. "You sound sort of experienced and just a wee bit bitter. Don't tell me that with your wealth, beauty, et cetera, anyone has had the temerity to offer you phony affection," she chided, and instantly regretted her impulse.

"Oh, I'm human," Irene answered dully. "Believe it or not, Marshall, when I was your age I wasn't hard to take, only I was without experience. I was naïve as a five-year-old and just about as confiding, believing in Santa Claus and in the innate goodness of the animal known as man. But that's all old stuff now. Perhaps a girl needs at least one broken heart during her lifetime in order to take the later heartaches in stride. Perhaps it has made me more sensitive to the hurts of others. Maybe by becoming immune myself I can better deal with that menace, the handsome male doctor. Who knows?"

Kathy Marshall stared out at the hurrying cars for a long moment before she said softly, "I've never known you to be bitter before, Irene. I'm sorry. But don't talk as if you were a hundred years old and a has-been, darling. You're still far from old, and a very handsome woman, and one of our best nurses, and what is more you know it."

The older nurse laughed apologetically. "I don't often go off the deep end like that, Kathy," she said, "but something happened last night that showed me, for a moment, the clay feet of a man I have—well, sort of idolized ever since I entered this hospital."

"Idolized?" Kathy whispered. "You idolized? I don't believe it."

"You don't have to," the other said quietly. "But will you bear with me? Will you take a tip from an old campaigner, Marshall?"

"Sounds ominous, Barker," the younger nurse answered ruefully. "What have I done or left undone now, for heaven's sake?"

"Oh, it has nothing to do with your work here."

"What then?"

"It's the new doctor—or should I say surgeon?—Gary MacDonald. Better give him a wide berth, darling."

Kathy Marshall's lovely face flushed, and her eyes sparkled with indignation. "But I scarcely know the man."

4

"O.K., O.K. So you scarcely know him, now, but I have a hunch that it won't be long——"

"You and your hunches!" Kathy scoffed. "I've told you a thousand times that I'm not interested in men, especially doctors."

"I know," Irene Barker agreed a bit skeptically, "I've heard all those arguments before. But you're young, you're sweet, and very, very lovely, and it just naturally follows that a young good-looking doctor will try to interest you. That's common sense and according to the laws of Mother Nature. You see, Kathy, I know. I'm just reminding you that the Chief doesn't approve of the new man. Maybe it's only conscience troubling him, but just the same——"

"His conscience? You mean the Chief's conscience, Barker? But why?"

"Oh it all happened before my time, Kathy, but the arrival of young MacDonald sort of revived the scandal, or perhaps a better term would be 'gossip.'" She paused for a moment to examine her well-manicured hands. "Have you met his mother? Gary's, I mean."

Kathy Marshall shook her bright head and stared at her friend in something like amazement. "Of course not. Why should I meet her?"

"Oh, for no special reason, only that she is very lovely even at middle age. And the Chief was once madly in love with her. I don't know if they were ever engaged but anyway she turned him down for Gary's father, a newcomer in Bostwick and a clever young surgeon. Blaine wasn't the man to take that lying down, you know. He maneuvered MacDonald off the staff here and was so disagreeable that Gary's father took his patients to Saint Luke's, on the North Side, and Memorial lost money. Not that it mattered so much because Memorial is heavily endowed and much better equipped and far more popular than Saint Luke's. People came from all over the state to have old Dr. Hartwick and his assistant, young Roger Blaine, operate on them. Blaine's clever, you know, and suave as an old-world courtier. But he didn't have long to wait for his revenge, if that was what he wanted. When Gary was about six or seven, his father was killed when his car went over an embankment one stormy night while he was returning from a late call. And although the way was now clear for Blaine to pick up where he left off, the widow would have nothing to do with him. That's the story being revived by the advent of Gary MacDonald."

"But—but the Chief wasn't guilty of anything, Irene," Kathy pointed out.

"Not legally, perhaps, but he made life pretty uncomfortable for the husband of his erstwhile sweetheart. Now we come to modern history. I happened to be in the linen room when the Chief and Channing came out of the doctor's scrubbery, and I heard the Resident say, 'Young MacDonald's a clever youngster, Chief. I think he will go far.' The Chief said nothing for a moment, and then he snarled—actually snarled, Kathy—'We'll give him plenty of rope, Doctor. He'll hang himself just as his father did before him. Bostwick Memorial isn't big enough for both of us, and I know who can quite easily be dispensed with.' Channning hemmed and hawed and then said as meekly as you please, 'Maybe you're right, Chief. Maybe you're right!'"

"I can't believe you heard that correctly, Irene," Kathy said. "There must have been something you missed that—"

"And so that's the reason I want you to fight shy of young MacDonald. You stand well with the Chief now, but don't crowd your luck. He intends to ruin the lad's career."

"You forget that his aunt, Mrs. MacDonald's sister, recently married Sam Bostwick himself. You know who he is. Practically owns this hospital. What Sam says goes, and I have a hunch that he intends Gary to be the next Chief of Staff."

"Oh, Irene, he's much too young for a job like that," Kathy pointed out. "Why, he can't be over thirty."

"All right," the other replied, "just wait and see. Well, I'll skip over to my room for a minute. I'll meet you at the foot of the stairs. Don't go in to dinner without me, Kathy, will you?"

Kathy promised to wait for her and returned to the window. Irene had spoken of idolizing someone here. The Chief? No, not the Chief. Could it be the Resident, Bob Channing? Dr. Channing was a bachelor—confirmed, according to reports. And just what was it that had occurred all those years ago that had made it possible for Dr. Blaine to force Gray's father from the staff of Memorial? She hadn't heard any of this in the year of

6

her work here in Bostwick. She wondered if Gary knew the story and, if so, just why he had decided to settle here and join the staff of Memorial. It was very puzzling, but after all it was none of her business, and she intended to put it completely from her mind.

She went slowly down the stairs and stood in the lower hall to wait for Irene. Nurses passed her, all headed for the dining room and dinner, but she remained standing, her back against the wall, and wishing her friend would hurry.

"Waiting for someone, Marshall?" a man's voice asked, and Kathy was startled at the sudden appearance of the Resident.

"Barker and I usually eat together, Dr. Channing," she answered.

He smiled and walked on toward the rear exit. He turned when he reached the small entrance hall to say, "Tell Barker I want to see her before she goes to 325 tonight. It's important, so don't forget."

"I won't forget, Dr. Channing," Kathy told him. So it was Bob Channing who had disappointed Irene, she mused, just as Irene ran down the stairs and joined her.

"I'm sorry to be a little late," Irene apologized as the two hurried along the long hall and down the short flight of steps to the big dining room. "Of course that Lois Bradley had some last-minute advice to give me. Who does she think she's kidding? And where does she get the idea she can tell any of us what we should and should not do? She's just one big pain in the neck, Marshall," she grumbled. "I bet I've forgotten more than she ever knew. I'm hungry and I hope there's plenty to eat tonight. Last night I had to fill up on chocolate wafers 325's visitors brought, and I'm well aware I should not eat sweets—especially chocolate. Something smells good anyway."

The two nurses found their places and were served hot soup, fresh rolls, thick slices of roast beef, and mashed potatoes, as well as gravy and vegetables.

"What, no salad, Agnes?" Irene asked the waitress. "Not that I'm especially heartbroken at the loss, but we're generally stuffed with a salad to save on the meat."

The waitress giggled. "We ran out of lettuce, Miss Barker," she explained, "but if you insist I can bring you

7

cabbage, though I'll tell you in confidence no one wants it. The cabbage is too old and is tough. I told Mrs. Bunting it wasn't fit to use when she bought that last crate, but you can't tell anyone anything around here."

"What are you muttering about, Agnes?" Miss Lowery, the Night Supervisor, demanded crispy from her place at the head of the table.

"What did I tell you?" was the parting shot of the waitress as she went back to the kitchen.

"You are so right, Agnes," Irene murmured as the girl disappeared.

"I don't care for raw cabbage anyway," Kathy remarked, "but I do like lettuce and all such fresh greens. I wonder why we never have watercress here. It's cheap and should be plentiful in the spring."

"Huh!" sniffed Irene scornfully. "You won't get watercress anyplace hereabout except in the very swankiest restaurants. I've only had it twice since I've been here."

"Oh, before I forget it, Barker," Kathy said hastily, "I met Dr. Channing just before I came in to dinner, and he asked me to tell you that he must see you before you go on duty tonight. What are you blushing for, Irene?" she teased as the other's face flamed. "Have I spoken out of turn or what? Oh, oh!"

As Kathy subsided, her friend gasped and then demanded testily, "What do you mean by that?"

"Just oh, oh!" Kathy answered demurely.

"I was a fool to talk so much," Irene muttered, but she received no response from the younger nurse, who seemed intent on finishing her dinner.

Irene Barker left the table before she had more than tasted her pudding, and Kathy smiled to herself. So that's the way the wind blows, is it? Well, Bob Channing had better watch his step if he wants to remain in Barker's good graces, she thought, as she finished her dinner and prepared to join the exodus, part of the staff leaving for an evening's pleasure but most of the nurses looking forward to night duty.

Ruth Holmes fell into step with Kathy as they reached the hall. "I'm sure glad it's you going into Receiving tonight instead of me," she said yawning. "I hate night duty anyway. I've had more than my share of it lately.

And do you know, I slept nine solid hours today and I'm still dead on my feet."

"Why don't you go back to bed then?" Kathy asked reasonably. "You're free tonight, aren't you?"

The other groaned. "Indeed I'm not, worse luck. Dan has tickets for the symphony tonight, and I'm almost certain I shall disgrace myself and him by sleeping through the entire performance. I hope I'm off night duty for a month at least. I hate every minute of it. Don't you?"

"No," murmured the other, shaking her head, "I've sort of got used to it now, so I don't seem to mind it. I don't know, however, about Receiving. It can be pretty exacting, although with Elliott on duty it isn't so bad."

"You're welcome to Elliott," Ruth Holmes muttered. "That stuffed shirt! I think he must have been dropped on his head when he was a baby, Marshall," she went on grimly. "Anyway, his sense of humor was misplaced. He considers life very real, and interning exceptionally earnest, and I find working with him the last word in boredom. I'd rather have either Clark or Burns. They, at least, can inject a bit of humor into the drab job of patching up broken bodies and dosing sick tummies."

"Just the same, Holmes," Kathy said, as she prepared to descend the stairs to Receiving. "I prefer Bill Elliott. He's competent, and he does his share of the work. Most of the others slide out of it whenever they can do so unobtrusively. S'long. See you at breakfast."

She walked briskly down the short flight and into the brightly lighted receiving room. Already there was activity apparent. A woman victim of a motor accident was propped up in a chair while Dr. Elliott and Della Morgan, a student nurse, completed her record. A man, driver of the other car, blood streaming down his face, stood anxiously watching and turned as Marshall entered.

"Make them hurry, Nurse," he pleaded. "She's hurt, maybe badly hurt, and they bother her with all that nonsense."

"She will be all right, sir," Kathy soothed. "What happened?"

"A truck sideswiped her, and she in turn rammed me. An accident, pure and simple, although I contend something should be done regarding trucks usurping the right of way regardless of traffic rules."

9

"Take care of him, Marshall," Dr. Elliott snapped, as he applied a medication to the long scratch on the side of the woman's face. So Kathy set about the routine of obtaining the necessary information and cleansing the cut close to the man's ear, and waited for Dr. Elliott, who turned to the man after the woman became calmer.

"You were lucky. Neither of you was badly hurt. How about the driver of the truck?"

The woman made an angry exclamation, and the man shook his head.

"The road was wet, Doctor," he said reasonably. "It was one of those heavy interstate trucks, this one loaded with what looked like steel pipes or rails. You probably have seen them passing here from time to time. It happened at the top of the hill. No doubt he saw Mrs.—this lady—coming toward him, and me following along behind. Probably he swerved a bit to give her plenty of room, and the truck slewed over and sideswiped her, and before I could brake my own car she in turn rammed me. I consider it an accident, pure and simple—unavoidable."

But the woman wouldn't have it that way. "I wish I could have got his license number," she stormed. "I'd sue his company for plenty and make him lose his job. There ought to be a law——"

"Be thankful you weren't badly injured," Dr. Elliott told her firmly. "It might have been really serious."

The man nodded in agreement, but the woman said shrilly, "Might have been! I shan't get over this shock in months, if ever. My nerves are completely shattered, not to mention the cut on my face—probably disfigure me for life——"

"How about your car? Was it damaged badly?"

"Not much beyond a bent fender as far as I could see." It was the man who spoke. "Mine is still in the ditch back there. I wonder if I could use a phone. I certainly can't get it out without help."

"And I have no intention of using what is left of my machine as a tow car," the woman said sourly. "I should like to use a telephone myself, at once, if it isn't asking too much. I want my husband to come, before I leave this place. I'm not at all satisfied with the treatment accorded me."

Dr. Elliott made no reply. He indicated the telephone on

a desk near the door, and the man called a service station. The woman called her husband, who promised to come as soon as a taxi could be obtained.

"You don't need a taxi," the woman told him sharply. "Ask the people next door to drive you up here. You've done plenty for them. . . . O.K., O.K., but step on it."

She returned to her seat, frowned at the others, and sniffed audibly when the man took out his wallet preparatory to paying for treatment. The doctor shook his head.

"We did nothing for you, sir. Glad to be of help. That's what this hospital is for, you know. Emergencies, when we can take care of them right here, are without charge. Glad you weren't hurt, and I hope your car isn't damaged too badly. Night!"

"I suppose he blames me because he went into the ditch," the woman muttered. "Didn't have his car under control—had no business driving so close to me anyway. It was that truckman's fault. I don't care what he says. But all men stick together." She got up and peered through the window at the highway some distance away. . . .

When a car turned into the hospital grounds, she took a belligerent attitude.

Her husband entered, looked at her, and said in a relieved voice, "Gosh, Mate, I'm glad you weren't hurt!"

It was the wrong thing to say, for the infuriated wife let fly, and while Dr. Elliott tried to smooth her ruffled feelings, the nurses went about the business of cleaning up.

The husband at last said tonelessly, "I saw a couple of men looking at the car outside. It seems to be all right."

"I suppose that Drake or whatever his name was had plenty of time to take the license number and will probably make us pay for any damage done to his car. I'll fight it!" she stormed.

"The insurance company will take care of everything, Mate," the husband told her, and he, too, took out his wallet. "What do we owe you, Doctor?" he asked quietly.

"Not a cent," his wife said quickly. "They didn't do anything for me worth paying for. I don't like this place, anyway. Let's go home, John. Well?" she added, as her husband lingered, his eyes questioning the doctor, who shook his head and smiled at the harassed man.

But John was reluctant to accept the doctor's verdict, and it was his wife who at last urged him from the room. Before the door closed, Kathy, who was nearest, heard her mutter vindictively, "Thanks for nothing!" and with her hand on the arm of her reluctant husband, the accident victim went into the night.

For the first time since she had worked with Dr. Elliott, Kathy heard his laugh, a deep infectious rumble that set both nures off into gales of mirth.

"Fancy being married to that shrew!" Della Morgan said. "Wasn't she the limit?"

"Probably shock," Kathy murmured. "Shock works queer tricks on people."

"You're right, Marhall," Dr. Elliott agreed, his approving gaze on Kathy. "However, the gentleman has my deepest sympathy. I wouldn't be in his shoes for all the gold in Fort Knox."

"It takes all sorts to make up this cockeyed world," the student nurse offered sententiously, and no one answered for the ambulance raced by the window and they knew that soon there would be work aplenty for them all.

CHAPTER TWO

A COLD October rain fell at night, and on this dark Friday morning it had resolved itself into a steady disconsolate drizzle. Over in another part of the city, Dana Adams, preparing to leave for work, drank the last of the coffee her grandmother brought to her and said warningly, "Listen, Gram, no marketing for you today. You stay right at home and let Butch get what you need.

"I don't like him to use the car when it's so wet and slippery, Dana." Mrs. Hammond sighed. "He's careful, but you know the condition of our tires, and accidents happen so quickly. I don't know if he will consent to walk, to carry whatever things I may find I need. And don't forget the plant I promised to give Mrs. Potter. Poor soul, it is so hard for her to be confined to the house. I know it's right on your way or I wouldn't even mention it in such weather. It is very trying, I know——"

"Oh, I don't mind it, Gram," the girl answered. "Don't worry about me, and if Butch makes a kick about the marketing I'll take care of it—and of him, too." She grinned, slipping into galoshes and raincoat, pulling the hood snugly over her head. "No, no, darling. I don't need an umbrella," she protested. "I despise the things. Remember what I told you, Gram. You stay right home today, and if that pain in your knee isn't better tomorrow I'm going to call the doctor. No sense in letting it go any longer. Good-by, darling. Be careful and don't work too hard. Pete should be home from college sometime this morning. Have him call me at the office." She laughed whimsically. "I want to hear the lad's voice."

The front door closed behind her, and she walked briskly down the steps and along the wet street, humming softly to herself as she avoided the puddles. Somehow the wet against her face felt good. She had always enjoyed walking in the rain, and, while there had been too much wet weather to suit the majority, Dana made no complaints. To her, life was wonderful; each day a glorious adventure, a mystery she was eager to solve.

Dana Adams was just an average girl who enjoyed her work, her fun, and the people with whom she came in daily contact. She was beautiful only as all youth is beautiful. She possessed a pleasing personality, a charming voice, and a pair of dancing feet of which her young brothers were inordinately boastful. While her somewhat sedate grandmother, with whom she lived, frowned at times at the demands made on the girl to dance at entertainments, she kept her peace, feeling sure that Dana would never allow herself to be exploited or her gift corrupted.

Dana was taller than average, slender, with dark curls and melting brown eyes that were perhaps her best feature and, as Butch used to say, "could pull the heart out of a mummy." Her color was good; her manner reserved yet independent. In fact she was very much like thousands of girls with jobs the country over. She was a favorite at the plant where she worked and was always willing to help out at any time, which fact no doubt added to her popularity.

This wet October morning she was greeted from time to time by passers-by and replied for the most part with a lifted hand and a quick smile. She approached the building in which her grandmother's friend lived and pressed the bell. The catch on the door was released, and she walked up one flight to the second floor, where Mrs. Potter's daughter met her. She had evidently been crying, for her eyes and nose were red and she still sniffed occasionally.

"Oh," she said, on seeing Dana, "I thought it might be Joe home again. He went out so cross this morning that— is this the plant Mrs. Hammond promised Mother, Dana?" Tears flowed again. "Mother went to the hospital—Memorial—last night. She had a bad spell, and the doctor advised it. Poor Mother! She didn't want to go, the expense, you know, but I told Joe—but you don't want to listen to my troubles, do you? I wish I could get away to take it to her today, but little Joey has a croupy cold and I can't leave him. Don't ever get married, Dana," she said fiercely and turned away, leaving the plant still in Dana's hands.

"Listen, Judith," Dana called, through the partly open door, "I'll take this to Memorial for you. I'm sure I can get a few minutes, and the bus runs right by the plant. Don't give it a thought, Judith. I'll stop in later and let you know how your mother is. I must run. Don't venture outside, it's a wicked day." To herself she added, as she went out into the drizzle, which somehow had increased rather than diminished despite the radio announcer's prediction, "Only I like it."

It was perhaps an hour later that she left her desk and, once more in raincoat and galoshes, picked up the plant and stood at the curb waiting for a bus which should be along any minute. She hadn't long to wait and climbed board, smiling at the driver who looked anything but happy but who couldn't refrain from meeting smile with smile.

"I want to get off as near as possible to Bostwick Memorial," Dana said, from her seat near the driver. "Shall I have far to walk?"

"Maybe a block. You should have taken the East Avenue bus—goes right past the hospital," the man replied. "What a day—what a day!"

Dana laughed. "Bad driving?" she asked.

"Wicked," the driver replied succinctly.

People got on and others stepped off and all looked disgruntled and unhappy, and Dana wondered why the weather should have the power to control one's disposition.

Bostwick Memorial looked almost forbidding as she left the bus and walked the short distance to the main entrance. She wasn't too familiar with this particular hospital. It was much the larger and certainly the better known of the two in Bostwick. Dr. Blaine, the Chief of Staff, was a

14

famous surgeon, and people came from miles around to have him operate. Gram had told her that Mrs. MacDonald's son had come here in the capacity of consulting surgeon, and Gram had looked sort of queer when she made the announcement. Dana had forgotten that Mrs. MacDonald had a son. After graduation from high school, she had thought rather seriously of entering the nurses' training school here and later, when that fell through, of becoming a nurses' aide, but she had never gotten around to it. Somehow her free time seemed so completely occupied. Now, as she entered the foyer of the huge hospital, she felt a tiny regret that she had allowed the opportunity to slip past.

There was a large circular desk on one side of the big hall into which she went, and one of the women sitting there moved closer as Dana entered, the heavy door closing silently behind her.

"May I see Mrs. Potter, please?" Dana asked quietly. "I believe she was brought here last night. I am here in her daughter's place."

"Just a minute," the young woman answered and reached for a card index. "She has room 416, fourth floor. Take the elevator at the end of this hall. Just step inside and press the button marked four."

Dana, who needed no advice about operating an automatic elevator, walked swiftly along the long hall and into the elevator, which had just that moment returned to the first floor, letting out several nurses and a white-coated young man who was grinning from ear to ear and whom Dana put down as one of the fresh internes she had heard the girls deride.

The door of 416 was ajar, and Dana pushed it wider. It was a small room containing a narrow bed, a dresser, and one chair. The window was narrow and gave a minimum of light. Mrs. Potter, looking frail and depressed, was propped up on pillows and showed little or no interest as Dana slipped into the room.

"Good morning, Mrs. Potter!" the girl said softly. "Are you feeling better this morning? Gram sent you the plant she promised. Look, isn't it pretty? She has nursed it for weeks until it was just right. I'll put it here where you can see it. May I sit down for a moment, or are you too tired for visitors this morning?"

15

"Dana! Dana! You dear girl!" the woman cried, her eyes filling with grateful tears. "I didn't have my glasses and didn't recognize you at first. How is your grandmother, Dana? Is her knee still bothering her? She's a lucky, lucky woman, my dear, to have her home and such devoted grandchildren. It is a terrible thing to reach the point where one is no longer needed or wanted. Hand me my spectacles. I want to see you and the plant. Oh, it is lovely! And so are you, my dear. Have you seen Judith? Poor girl! Joe is very unreasonable. She has it hard, though with me out of the way it should be a bit easier."

"Judith misses you, Mrs. Potter," Dana told her, feeling as if she would like to wring Joe Barrow's neck.. "She couldn't come this morning because Joey has a cold, and this weather doesn't help any. She will probably come later, maybe when Joe comes home from work and can stay with the baby."

A nurse entered, eyed Dana for a moment, then proceeded to take the patient's temperature, fingers on pulse and watch in hand. Dana watched her, fascinated. Nursing had always intrigued her, and once again she experienced a feeling of regret that she hadn't followed that long-ago urge to enter training school. Of course it wasn't too late yet, she was still young, but she loved her job at the plant. She shook her dark head as if to dispose of that old dream.

"Please don't remain very long," the nurse advised as she shook down the thermometer and prepared to leave the room. "Mrs. Potter should be sleeping. She had a rather poor night, although," she added, "you are undoubtedly better for her right now than sleep." She smiled as she departed.

"Oh, don't go, Dana," the woman pleaded. "I get so very lonesome, so depressed. Must you leave now?"

"I ought to, Mrs. Potter," the girl said regretfully. "You know I'm a working woman, and while I was given permission to come here I feel sure they expect me back very soon. And I promised Judith to stop in later and tell her how you are. Better, aren't you? Smile for Dana, darling, and I can tell her that. I'm sure she will be glad to know."

Suddenly she bent down and pressed her cool young cheek against the withered one on the pillow.

"You'll come in again, won't you, Dana?" the woman

16

begged, and Dana promised. She went out and walked down three flights of stairs to the main floor, eager, for some reason, to leave the place, leave the unhappiness and despair that seemed to take up the entire space.

Outside, the drizzle had subsided but the sky was leaden and the air wet. Dana wondered if she dared take the time to walk back to the office. She had been gone less than an hour, but it was two miles at least to the plant, so she boarded the bus and was back at her desk within a few minutes of the hour she had requested for her errand.

"How did you find your friend, Dana?" Mr. Wentworth asked, when, notebook in hand, she entered his office a few minutes later. "Better, I hope."

"I really don't know," Dana replied, her face troubled. "She was very depressed and rather worried about her daughter and the baby who has a cold. Do you know, I never felt that either Mrs. Potter or the Barrows were poor. Maybe they're not, as far as money goes, but there seems to be a sad lack of affection and consideration, one for the other. It struck me forcibly at the apartment and later when I talked with Mrs. Potter, who happens to be a friend of Gram's. But"—she smiled apologetically—"it might be the weather."

"Could be," the man agreed. "But tell me, Dana, just who is this Barrow? The name sounds familiar. Do I know him?"

"Probably. He's in politics—what do you call it?— ward boss, alderman, something of the sort. But he was a master plumber when Judith Potter married him. A big handsome fellow, although somehow I don't like him." She grinned whimsically at the man opposite, who shook his head.

"Just as well you don't, Dana," he said. "I imagine young Dalton might object to sharing your affections with anyone. What are you blushing for? Anything serious there? As if it were any of my business."

"Absolutely not, Mr. Wentworth," the girl replied. "Nick and I have been pals ever since dancing-school days. He's like a brother to me, nothing more." She sat forward in her chair and fingered a pencil suggestively.

"O.K., O.K.," the man said. "We should hate losing you, but we know that of course we must some day. Now for work."

17

His dictation was clear and rapid, and Dana filled her book and reached for the additional one with which she had armed herself. Mr. Wentworth was the firm's correspondent, and Dana was used to dozens of letters at each sitting. She liked and admired the junior member of the firm and enjoyed working with him.

Not all the letters were ready for his signature when the five o'clock whistle blew, but the most important ones were, and she laid them on his desk and said, "There are several more, Mr. Wentworth. Shall I stay and finish them tonight?"

"Absolutely not," he replied firmly. "I'll sign these, and you see that they get off tonight, will you? That new mail boy somehow manages to get out of here promptly when the whistle blows. And yet he's a good lad. We all like him. Go back to your desk and close up for the night, Dana. Might as well get ready to leave. I'll bring these out to you, and you can take them along with you to the substation. They should go out tonight."

"I'll do that, Mr. Wentworth," Dana said and left the room.

Dana was later than usual getting home that evening, and Mrs. Hammond had dinner about ready to serve when she came in. Her brother, Peter, met her at the door and caught her in a bear hug, lifting her high in the air.

"Gee, Dana, but you're a sight for sore eyes! How's business this lousy weather? Why do you let your boss impose on you? Here you are, almost an hour late. I don't approve of this overtime, sis, and I think I shall take steps? Big fellow? Bigger than I am? I'd better know the facts before I tackle him." He straightened himself to his slim six feet two and spread his arms wide. "Tell me the worst, Dana.

Dana giggled. "Don't be a dope, Peter," she admonished. "Mr. Wentworth is tops. He's kind, generous and very understanding. They don't come any better than John Wentworth. I love working with him."

"Sa-ay," the young man demanded, eying his sister suspiciously. "How old is this superman? Does Grafn know about this—this crush?"

"Let's see," Dana mused, wrinkling her pretty nose. "I imagine he must be in his middle forties—and to ease your mind, my inquisitive young brother, he is married and the adoring father of four children, two girls and twin boys. Anything else?"

"Still, at that," Peter muttered, his face downcast as if he were really worried, "the forties are considered a dangerous age for males, you know. They're always making grabs for remnants of their lost youth," He caught her hand and grinned down at her. "Gram's fit to be tied. Dinner's been ready this long time, and I'm starved."

"Where's Butch?" Dana asked. The youngest Adams was generally very much in evidence when Peter was home.

"Butch is making himself useful," Peter told her, tongue in cheek. "I found it necessary to lecture him when I got home because he raised a holler when Gram suggested he do the week's marketing. 'Why don't we have a decent car? What do we have a telephone for? Why can't Dana do it during her noon hour?' And so on and so on. As man of the family I felt it incumbent upon me to point out his duty to his grandmother, his sister, and the well-being of the family in general. Consequently, sis, Butch is sulking but he's helping Gram put on the dinner. That's one thing gained. But don't let on that I told you any of this. We're having halibut steak tonight, and you know how I go for that. Do you suppose my lecture had anything to do with Butch adding that to the market list? I love that kid, Dana, obstreperous as he is."

"Of course you do, and so do I. Come on, Pete. What are we waiting for? You're not the only one who happens to be starved."

The kitchen was warm and bright, and as Dana kissed her grandmother's flushed cheek she patted the head of the younger brother affectionately as he stooped to take the fish from the oven.

"You're late, Dana," the old lady said quietly. "I think you work too hard. Such long hours! Did you see Amelia Potter? How is she? And Judith, poor girl, how is she making out?"

"After grace, honey, I'll tell you everything," Dana replied and bowed her dark head as her grandmother repeated the familiar prayer.

"We thank Thee, Lord, for this Thy food.
Bless it to our bodies and us to Thy service,
and make us ever grateful. Amen."

The big kitchen was the favorite dining place these

cool autumn days, and, except when more than the family dined with them, all their meals were eaten at the kitchen table, with mats taken the place of cloths to lessen laundry expense. Sometimes Mrs. Hammond demurred at what she contended was a lack of refinement, but the children jeered at her. Why give herself more work, carrying dishes and food to the big dining room? Since Tilly, the hired girl who used to work for them, had married and gone into a home of her own, Mrs. Hammond had done her own housework with what aid could be obtained from her three grandchildren. They all loved the kitchen, and eating in it certainly did reduce the work and the expense.

Dana told of the day's experiences, of finding Mrs. Potter in the hospital and of her delight in the visit and her gratitude for the plant. She didn't mention finding Judith Barrow in tears and of her conjecture as to the Barrow's marital and financial status. Why worry Gram? The meal was eaten with enjoyment, and before the dessert of custard and applesauce was reached Butch's sulks were forgotten and he told hilarious tales of marketing—most of which, they surmised, were purely imaginary. Butch was a born mimic and saw humor in the most humdrum of incidents.

"Butch and I will take care of the dishes, Gram," Dana offered, as the meal ended. "Won't we Butch?" she added experimentally.

"Humph!" the boy growled. "Why ask? I seem to be the fall guy around here."

"Oh, go roll your hoop!" his brother told him, ignoring Dana's warning headshake. "I'll help Sis with the dishes, if she'll let me wash."

"I said I'd do 'em, didn't I?" Butch shouted. "Dana and I almost always do 'em. Nothing unusual about that. You go visit your blonde, big boy."

"What blonde?" Peter demanded shortly.

"Maybe she's a brunette, then, I wouldn't know," Butch jeered, and dodged the poke his brother threatened.

Mrs. Hammond and Pete left the room, and the two remaining made short work of the dishwashing. The telephone in the hall sounded several times, and Dana realized that Pete's friends were evidently aware of his homecoming. And then as the girl was hanging up the last wet towel, her grandmother called to Butch, who had in the meantime taken the opportunity to slip out on affairs of his own. Friday night was his night at the Y, and he seldom missed one. Dana went into the living room, where she found her grandmother knitting before a glowing fire. Pete was nowhere in sight, Probably he, too, had gone out.

"Butch went out, Gram," Dana said. "What can I do for you? And where is Pete?"

"Someone came for him. He promised to return very soon, and perhaps I can wait, but there is a glass of black currant jelly on the cupboard top shelf that I feel sure Mrs. Reynolds will enjoy; her appetite is so poor these days. It is the last one we have. I didn't make any this year. Black currants were scarce, or at least I wasn't able to get any. You know where I mean, Dana? The cold room——" but Dana was already running down the basement stairs.

Some minutes elapsed before Mrs. Hammond heard the low cry for help. She ran to the stairs and peered down; then, forgetting her stiff knee, she hurried to the big cement-floored basement and at the foot of the stairs found Dana, struggling frantically to get to her feet. The old lady felt a sudden premonition that the girl was badly hurt.

"Don't struggle, Dana," she urged. "Try to lie quiet . . . I'll be right back," she promised, as she ran back and reached for the telephone, calling frantically to Central to send either the police or firemen, trying desperately to explain that her granddaughter had fallen in the basement and there was no one to help. She dialled the family doctor only to find he was out, but Mrs. Morse, his wife, promised to find him.

"We'll send someone," she assured Mrs. Hammond. "Can I help?" But the old lady was no longer listening; she had hung up.

She tore the woolen afghan from the couch and again went down the stairs to try to slip it beneath the injured girl by kneeling on the cold floor, quite oblivious of her own stiff knee.

"Oh, Gram, Gram!" the girl cried, biting her lips to keep back her terror. "I'm afraid I've broken my hip— my leg at least. It is useless. Oh, Gram, what shall I do?"

Suddenly the old lady became calm and strong. "Lie

right here, darling, and don't struggle or try to move. Help is coming very soon, and a doctor."

Even as she spoke there were sounds of hurrying feet on the floor above, and two young men in the uniform of the police came down the basement stairs. In an unbelievably short time and with infinite gentleness they lifted the injured girl on an improvised stretcher and carried her up the stairs to the living room couch. And the frantic call Mrs. Hammond had sent to the family doctor was relayed to young Dr. MacDonald, who arrived almost at once.

Just as the ambulance raced into the quiet street, Peter and Butch reached the house. Dr. MacDonald told them briefly just what the conditions were and supervised the transferring of the injured girl to the ambulance, into which Pete promptly climbed.

"I'm going with you, Sis," he whispered into the girl's ear. "No one's going to hurt you while I'm around."

The accompanying intern smiled and assured them there was no intention of hurting anyone. "She'll be all right," he volunteered. "Doc MacDonald sure knows his business. She's in darned good hands."

Butch and Mrs. Hammond wanted to go with Dana, but the doctor helped them both into his own car, and they preceded the ambulance to Bostwick Memorial by several minutes. It was Gary MacDonald who turned off the lights, saw that the fire screen was in place, and then handed the front door key to Mrs. Hammond, put on the night latch, and slammed the front door. He hoped the other doors were locked, but there wasn't time to investigate. He wanted to be at the hospital before the ambulance arrived. He was.

CHAPTER THREE

THE AMBULANCE HAD stopped before the service entrance, and the stretcher had been wheeled into the elevator, when Butch Adams went along the corridor to Receiving, his face white and his dark eyes wide with tragedy. Dr. Elliott went to him and urged him to a seat.

"What happened?" he asked gently. "Accident? A member of your family? Tell us about it." Kathy Marshall, pen in hand, waited for the information.

"It's my sister," Butch said, his voice husky with feeling. "She fell, and the doctor says her hip is broken.

They've taken her to the X-ray room to find out just how bad it is." He choked. "Gram and my brother Pete are up there with her. They made me come here."

"Go ahead," the doctor urged. "Give us the name, age, and any other particulars the nurse must have. Or has the doctor all the information that is necessary for our records? Who is your doctor?"

"MacDonald," the boy said. "Our own doctor, Morse, was out on a case and couldn't be located and—and his wife called MacDonald. Dana's twenty-two. She's a stenographer over at the Plow Works. I—I want to go to her, Doctor. She's hurt bad."

Kathy's eyes were soft with pity as she watched the boy's face. "Your sister will be all right," she said at last, softly, as the lad fought for control. "She is in the right place and in good hands. I'm sure of that. Can you give me her full name, address, and the names of her parents?"

The boy gulped and then said raggedly, "They're both dead. We live with Gram—Mrs. Hammond—over on Sedgewick Drive. You prob'ly know Gram. Everyone does." The nurse looked at Dr. Elliott, who nodded and waved a hand as if to say the interview was over. The boy got to his feet and started for the door.

"Wait a minute," the doctor said. "I'll find out which room she is to have, and you can wait there for her. You say Mrs. Hammond is with her, and your brother? Let's see then, you must be——" he paused.

The boy answered a bit impatiently, "Oh, I'm Butch—Paul Adams. My brother Pete happened to be home from college for the week end—he goes to Hamilton. Good thing he was, too, for Gram just about collapsed after it happend. Dana's always rushing around doing things for her, and this time she went down to the basement for something Gram wanted, and somehow or other she slipped and fell off two steps right onto the cement floor. If I'd been home I could have carried her right upstairs, but Gram had already called a couple of cops and they seemed to know just how to move her without hurting her worse. Seems as though cops are trained in first aid, or something. Do you think she will be all right, Doctor? Dana loves to dance, play tennis, swim—she'll want to die if she's going to be a cripple."

Dr. Elliott patted the boy's shoulder and urged him

23

toward the door. "Of course she won't be a cripple," he said comfortingly. "People break hips every day; most of them recover completely without even a limp. Your sister is very young. She'll be all right, take it from me. Now run along. Take the elevator to the fourth floor and go straight to room 407 and wait. I'm sure you will find your grandmother already there, perhaps your sister and brother also. Night, son."

"No need to bother him with questions, Marshall," he said to the nurse, as he returned to the room. "While Mrs. Hammond is by no means wealthy, she's good as gold as far as financial risk is concerned, and I think the three Adams youngsters inherited some money from their parents. Probably a trust fund. But they are good people, and the Chief need have no qualms about their paying the bill."

He said the last more to himself rather than to the others, and Kathy Marshall couldn't repress the feeling that his tone held bitterness. So Dr. Elliott was evidently no blind worshiper of the Chief of Staff as were a few of the others here at Memorial. And yet she may have imagined it all. Perhaps it was due to the conversation she had had with Irene Barker. She wondered if Dr. Blaine were in the X-ray room, and how he and young MacDonald met the situation.

But as it happened, Dr. Blaine was out of town on this particular night. One of his colleagues was visiting in a neighboring city and had called him for a conference, so that it was the Resident, Dr. Channing, who assisted the technician and Gary MacDonald in their examination. Dana Adams appeared to be completely unaware of what went on around her. She lay on the table, white and still, her eyes closed, her features immobile. The doctors murmured together with the technician in the nearby dark room. Dr. MacDonald spoke as they viewed the X-ray pictures.

"A good break if there ever was one," he said softly. "We'll use the Roger Anderson splint. Should work perfectly. Get her to bed and better send the family home. Who is floor nurse on the fourth, Doctor?" he asked the Resident.

"Porter. Jean Porter. Fine nurse, Doctor," Dr. Channing answered. "How about specials for the first twenty-

24

four or forty-eight hours? Hard to get, but I think we could manage if you think it best."

Dr. MacDonald shook his head. "I don't believe that it's at all necessary. The girl is young and healthy, and the floor nurse should be able to look after her. I imagine she will sleep all night and even part of tomorrow, when we shall take care of that hip. After all—well, we'll see." He turned to a nurse who had just entered. "Get her to bed—er—Baldwin. If you need help, the floor nurse is available. And by the way, see that her family leaves. The patient will undoubtedly sleep for hours. I'll look in on her during the night." He turned, and the two doctors left the room together.

But Dana Adams knew nothing of what went on around her and did not even dimly recognize her adored grandmother or either her young brothers who waited anxiously for her return. The nurse motioned them to leave the room, and in the dim corridor she told them the patient was asleep and would undoubtedly sleep all night, and for them to go home and get some rest. The operation would be in the morning, and they could come to the hospital in the afternoon; and for them not to worry, for Miss Adams was going to be all right.

Butch looked almost belligerent as the nurse talked in a quiet impersonal voice, and it was only Pete's hand on his arm that kept him from telling her that he intended staying right where he was.

"Gram should be in bed, Butch," the elder boy said softly. "She looks fit to drop, and you know Dana would never forgive us if Gram should get sick while she's away. Come on, let's take Gram home. We can't do anything for Dana hanging around here."

"How long will she have to stay here?" Butch demanded of the nurse, who had looked approvingly at the elder brother.

"That depends, of course," was the nurse's noncommittal reply. "But after the casts are removed it should not be too long, and then you will have the job on your hands of teaching her to walk all over again. She is fortunate in having two brothers for that job."

"Teach her to walk!" Butch showed his horror. His graceful, dancing sister not able to walk until taught! The idea was horrible. He couldn't bear it.

25

His brother said soothingly, "Of course, dope. But it won't take long. She'll help. Dana won't ever let a little thing like a broken hip keep her down. Not Dana. Come on, let's go home. Thank you, Nurse," he said as they moved toward the elevator.

And as the trio walked down the long dim corridor, Anita Baldwin watched them with a feeling almost of envy. How wonderful to have two such splendid brothers as Pete and Butch! Butch. She grinned wryly to herself. No doubt his real name was much too sedate or fanciful to suit that young gentleman's requirement. But she liked them both and the grandmother was charming—so quiet, and sort of controlled, and yet anyone could see with half an eye that she was worried sick. This Dana Adams was a lucky girl even with a broken hip.

It was later that same evening that Dr. MacDonald stopped at the Hammond home on Sedgewick Drive. The house was lighted, so he knew the family was up—no doubt worrying about the girl. He had sensed the anxiety of the grandmother and brothers of the victim of the accident and was taking time out of his busy life to try to ease the situation.

"Oh, Dr. MacDonald!" Butch cried, as he opened the door to admit him. "Is Dana worse?"

"Easy, Butch," the visitor advised, his hand on the boy's shoulder. "I stopped in to see if I could relieve your anxiety a bit. Make things more understandable to Mrs. Hammond. Are you all here?"

"Living room," Butch told him, gesturing across the hall where light gleamed from a glowing grate fire. "But——"

"There isn't a thing for you to worry about," the doctor told him, as they walked into the room. He spoke to the others and drew a chair close to that of Mrs. Hammond. "I thought I could perhaps show you exactly what has happened to Miss Adams and just what we propose to do for her."

He took a prescription pad from his pocket and with his fountain pen began to draw a picture. All three watched him closely. It was evident that he was no artist, although he knew his anatomy.

"Now this is what has happend to Miss Adams," he said, as he paused for a moment. "You see, the ball of the

26

thighbone was broken clean from the femur something like this, allowing the femur to slip about two and a half to three inches into the thigh, thus shortening the right leg that amount." He passed the paper to Mrs. Hammond, who nodded with compressed lips.

Reclaiming the paper he went on, using his pen swiftly. "Now this is what we are going to do. It is called the Roger Anderson splint and has proved extremely successful in numberless cases such as this. Plaster casts are put on the *uninjured* leg, in this case the left one, from the thigh down; on the leg with the fractured hip the cast extends only from below the knee. The left leg will serve as traction. A post is inserted through the ankle bone of the injured right leg, and the key on the left leg is turned occasionally and so gradually pulls the shortened femur back into position to join the ball. The feet are fixed in what we call stirrups, which in turn are secured to the foot of the bed, thus insuring absolute and necessary immobility. X rays are taken periodically in order to watch the progress. Do you see? Of course you realize these sketches are exaggerated. I just wanted you to understand the situation."

Mrs. Hammond bit her lip and after a moment said, "But that post through her anklebone. Won't that hurt? Is that necessary?"

The doctor smiled patiently. "No, she won't feel it then or ever. We shall see to that. She won't even feel the occasional turning of the key that will eventually bring the femur back where it belongs. I assure you, Mrs. Hammond," he went on earnestly, "the entire proceeding is as nearly painless as it is possible to make it. Of course, she will have to endure the inactivity of lying in bed—mostly on her back, except when the nurses turn her over on her side, which they will do after a time. It won't be easy for her, but I have a notion it will be much harder for you to endure than it will be for the patient, who appears to be a resourceful and understanding young woman."

Butch, who had the doctor's sketch in his hands, broke the tension. He held the paper at arm's length for a moment, then turned to his grandmother and said disgustedly, "I guess you never saw our Dana's legs, Doctor. She has beautiful legs. Not much like the stumps here." He slapped the paper with his hand.

27

Dr. MacDonald grinned ruefully. "I'm not much of an artist, Butch. That sketch was just to give you people an idea of the method we propose using tomorrow. I'm sure your sister is beautiful in every respect."

"Don't be such a dope!" Peter Adams admonished his younger brother, but he saw that his grandmother's lips were no longer compressed and that even a tiny smile hovered there.

She spoke, her voice somewhat tremulous. "You were very kind to stop in and explain all this to us, Dr. Mac-Donald, and we feel sure you will do everything possible for our girl. She is very dear to us all, and we want her to have the best of care. You will see to that, won't you?"

"I certainly shall," the young man said earnestly. "I was in to see her before I came here, and she was sleeping quietly."

"And nurses?" Mrs. Hammond asked. "I know they are scarce but——"

"Special nurses are not at all necessary, Mrs. Hammond. Your granddaughter is young, there nothing at all complicated about this, and I am sure the nurses on duty on that floor will take excellent care of her. You may run in tomorrow afternoon for a visit, if you like. I am sure you will all feel relieved to see that she is bearing up remarkably well. I have great confidence in her." He got to his feet, and all three, grandmother and the two boys, accompanied him to the door.

It was late when the doctor left the Hammond home, and he turned his car toward his mother's house. He was tired. It had been a strenuous day, and already he had begun to feel the enmity and lack of cooperation of Memorial's Chief of Staff. His mouth hardened. Well, he was sure of one thing. Blaine, in spite of his pull, was not going to oust him from his hard-won position as consulting surgeon at the hospital. And even without the influence of Aunt Edith's husband, who had urged him to hold up his head and to take no abuse from any member of the staff, Gary MacDonald had no intention of toadying to anyone, least of all to the Chief of Staff. Let him do his worst. And yet, being a fair-minded young man, he acknowledged the older man's ability. He was a fine surgeon, even if so arbitrary and sharp-tongued that he often left nurses who worked with him in tears and assisting doctors boiling with rage. In spite of the fact that no one really liked the man, they all agreed he knew his job and was unusually successful.

Gary McDonald knew Dr. Blaine had fought his appointment to the hospital. He had heard the old story of Blaine's enmity for his father and the tricks he had used to oust him from the staff. And that knowledge served only to strengthen his determination to remain. He had no least desire to antagonize the Chief, but neither did he intend becoming a yes man for the sake of holding his job. He didn't have to, thank heaven. But somehow he hoped the Chief would remain away from the hospital until after the Adams hip operation. He worked better without close supervision, especially Blaine's.

He locked the garage and walked along the brick walk to the back door. A light burned in the kitchen, and he hoped his mother had not remained up for him as she so often did. The kitchen was empty, however, although there was a glass of milk and a plate of sandwiches on the table. He went into the front hall, hung up his coat, and saw that the rest of the house was dark except for a light upstairs, no doubt in his mother's room. The milk was cold and the sandwiches appetizing, and he suddenly discovered that he was hungry. His mother joined him as he finished the last one.

"You should be in bed and asleep," he admonished her, as she drew the kitchen rocker nearer. "I shall have to prescribe for you if this keeps on."

"Oh, I get plenty of sleep, Gary," she replied, "and I wanted to ask about little Dana Adams. How is she? Her grandmother told me she had fallen and broken a hip. That poor child with her dancing feet and sunny disposition! Just how serious is it? Will she be all right?"

Her son laughed at her. "So many questions," he chided, "but I think I can answer them by saying 'yes' to that last. She is young and healthy and should come through the ordeal with a minimum of impairment. You know, Mother, I don't seem to remember the family at all. Should I?"

His mother shook her head. "You have been away for so long that children, probably too young for you to notice before, have simply grown up—all except Butch, who was a baby when his parents were killed. He is still a boy, seventeen or thereabouts, headstrong of course as all teen-agers are inclined to be. But you should remember Martha Hammond, Gary."

The young man shook his head. "I don't seem to. I like her, and I like the boys, too. I don't know much about the girl. She was asleep when I stopped in at the hospital tonight, but she seems like a sensible young woman. Butch says she's a stenographer somewhere in town."

"Martha Hammond is very well thought of here in Bostwick, Gary," his mother pointed out. "Not much money, but enough for their needs, I suspect. I believe the children's parents left a trust fund, but I really don't know much about their finances. I suppose Dana's hospitalization will cost considerable?"

"I really can't say," her son answered. "My own bill won't be exorbitant, I'll promise you that, but hospitalization costs plenty these days."

"How long will she have to stay in the hospital?" his mother wanted to know.

"Possibly ten or twelve weeks. At least until the casts are off. I really can't say at the moment. But I'm sure the family will want her home just as soon as she can be released. We are using the Roger Anderson splint method, you know. You must have heard of that."

"Yes," his mother replied. "Finished? Better run up to bed, darling. You need your rest. You are working far too hard."

Gary pooh-poohed at the very thought but snapped off the light and followed his mother upstairs. It was good to be at home, and if a tiny whisper of dissatisfaction marred his happiness he pushed it away and slipped into bed with a sigh of complete relaxation. Blaine could attend to his own affairs and leave him to attend to his. And on this specious thought Gary MacDonald dozed having no idea that he might be the subject of discussion among the nurses, many of whom he had come to know and to admire. Marshall, especially, was both attractive and efficient. He believed her first name was Katherine. Some called her Kathy. He liked her, maybe——

A long tired sigh escaped him, and he slept.

CHAPTER FOUR

WHILE THE WINTER WAS NOT A particularly severe one, the days were dark and the sun seemed to have taken a leave of absence, for it showed itself but seldom during the weeks that followed a dreary October. Everyone wished for snow for Thanksgiving, or at least for Christmas. How terrible it would be not to have a white Christmas! There were a few snow flurries around Thanksgiving, but then the second week of December brought a real blizzard.

Time dragged for most of the patients in Bostwick Memorial, especially for those confined to their beds, and so it was with relief—almost eagerness—that nurses paid brief visits to room 407 where Dana Adams, with her ready smile and pleasant, sometimes funny little greetings, met them.

"Honestly, Dr. Channing," one of the busy nurses told him on a particularly unpleasant morning, "I'm actually a new creature after my morning call on that girl. How does she do it? Is it true that she suffers no pain, simply has to endure inactivity?"

The Resident shook his head. "I doubt if she has had or will have any actual pain—discomfort, of course, but no pain. As to her continued good spirits, that, Morton, is due to a God-given ability to take what comes with cheerfulness, even gaiety. Then, too, she thinks of her grandmother, and the brothers who haunt the hospital, and she knows how they would suffer if she showed the white feather. Dana Adams is a wonderful girl. I admire her immensely, in fact we all do. She's good for us. I wish we had more patients like her."

The nurse shrugged as she left the Resident and walked on down the long corridor. Channing can talk all he wants to about her altruism, she mused, but to my way of thinking it's her youth and beauty—her luck in being born into the family she was—that she can thank for being the girl she is. Fancy an older woman, with little or nothing to look forward to, greeting each dreary day with a smile, with optimism as to the future. Channing with his smug theories is all wet.

She went on to the linen room, where she filled her arms with fresh bedding and forgot Channing, Dana Adams, and everything else, but somehow the day with its usual round of monotonous duties didn't seem so dreary or so uninteresting.

Dana watched eagerly for the coming of her beloved grandmother, who arrived each morning at ten bringing all the news of the family and the town in general. Later in the day, members of the office staff, the girls and boys with whom she worked at the Plow Works, dropped in for a few minutes' stay, and in the evening there was an occasional visit from her boss, Mr. Wentworth, or one of the other executives of the big plant. Her room was usually filled with flowers and plants, and when Gram came she took care of them; watering, picking off withered and dead leaves, and arranging them to give the patient the greatest pleasure. Butch dropped in from high school every afternoon, and each Sunday was a gala day in room 407.

And then, after a month of this, Dr. Blaine, the Chief of Staff, decided so much company was not good, either for the patient or the hospital in general, and imposed a drastic rule, curtailing visiting hours and limiting callers to two or three at a time, with shorter stays.

"But why, Dr. MacDonald?" Dana asked the young surgeon, after Gram and Butch had left far too soon to please either them or her. "I love having them here. It seems almost like being at home. I'm used to having people around me. Just why does Dr. Blaine object? We're not in the least noisy, and I'm sure it doesn't do me any harm."

The brown eyes were stormy with indignation as she stared at the young surgeon, who shook his head, a tiny smile of derision twisting his lips.

"Don't let it worry you, Dana," he told her. "After all, Dr. Blaine is boss here, you know, and what he says goes, almost always." He added the last more to himself than to the girl. "However, in a few weeks now we shall be removing those casts, and after that you can count the days until you go home. But let me tell you, my dear, we are going to miss you. You have been a wonderful patient, and the nurses tell me you do them good."

"Me? I do *them* good?" Dana asked.

The young man nodded. "You would be surprised if you could listen to the reports some of the nurses give. And do you know, I'm proud of you, and you are going to be all right. The X rays show that that runaway femur has come back home where it belongs, to be securely united with the deserted ball, and after a few weeks all that remains is for you to learn to walk once more and that, I am sure, won't take long. I had thought of seeing about a

32

walker for you, but your brothers vetoed the idea. Crutches, canes, and a walker are out. They intend to be your sole aids. I asked Peter how he could manage, since he's still in college, but he informed me there was a stand-in he could get, and he would be home every week end he possibly could. There are the Christmas holidays coming very soon now, and he intends utilizing that two weeks to good advantage. You're a lucky girl. Do you know it?"

"One of the nurses spoke to me about a walker, Doctor," Dana said, her brow puckering in a frown. "She told me Dr. Blaine insisted that I have one, but I happen to know of a boy—I think he was eight or nine—who used a walker under similar circumstances, and later it was necessary to put braces on his ankles and feet. He had come to depend on the walker and had allowed his ankles to weaken. And then we have a neighbor who after five years is still using a walker. No, Dr. MacDonald, I shall not use a walker, the big boss notwithstanding."

"Atta girl!" Gary MacDonald applauded. "Stick to it. Anyway, it will be some time yet until we need to think of that. I'll see you again."

Outside in the hall, he almost bumped into a nurse who was about to enter Dana's room. "Oh, hello, Marshall! Still in Receiving?"

Kathy Marshall shook her head. "Back on special work, Doctor," she told him. "I'm in 412, just down the hall. It's an interesting case. Do you know it?"

"Let's see, 412 must be young Latham. Smashup, wasn't it? The Chief mentioned the possibility of amputating a hand. How is he making out, Marshall? Elliott tells me he's an engineer. Too bad. I hope it can be saved."

Kathy's lips were pressed tightly together, and for a moment she didn't answer. Then she said, somewhat hotly, "He won't lose that hand if I can prevent it, Doctor. We had quite a time with his young brother last night. He threatened to kill the man who attempted to amputate his brother's hand and honestly, Dr. MacDonald, at the risk of losing my job I don't blame him. I have seen worse hands than Bob Latham's, and if we can keep the infection down —and I feel sure we can—there should be no amputation."

Gary MacDonald's face was grave. "Of course you realize there are cases where amputation is the quickest and surest road to recovery, Marshall?"

33

"Maybe," the nurse replied firmly, "but what has time to do with it when it means the man's whole future? He's only thirty, and his wife is worried to death. She begged me to save his hand, and I promised to try my hardest and I mean to. Dr. MacDonald, I wish you were on the case——" She bit her lip in embarrassment. "I mean," she stammered, "you're young and would understand his position. He told me he would rather die than lose his hand, and he really meant it. I'm going to fight, Doctor, and if I lose my job I'll lose it, that's all."

The young consulting surgeon smiled and patted her shoulder. "You won't lose your job, Marshall," he told her. "Just who are these Lathams? Money? Influence? Local people? I've been away from Bostwick so long that I've lost contact with the Bostwickians."

"I don't know a great deal about them, Doctor," the nurse said. "The younger brother threatened to call in specialists from New York, Boston, and Baltimore before anything drastic was done, and Dr. Elliott told him that the Chief was the best man in his line they could find but even that didn't convince him."

"I suppose not. Well, controlling the infection should delay any final decision, Marshall," he told her. "I suggest you carry on as you have been doing, and I'll have a talk with Dr. Elliott. He is certainly one member of the staff who thinks for himself. Good man, Elliott. I wish we had more like him. . . . I think you will find our patient in this room a credit to her surgeon and the hospital in general." He left her as Kathy pushed open the door of 407.

"I was hoping you could drop in this morning, Nurse," Dana said cordially. "But why aren't you sleeping? Aren't you on night duty?"

Kathy laughed. "Yes, I'm on night duty right on this floor, just down the hall a few doors from you. I've been kept so busy, though, that I haven't been able to stop in even for a minute. That's why I'm here now. Just to say 'hello' and find out how things are going with you."

"Oh, I'm O.K., or as O.K. as one can be trussed up like a Thanksgiving turkey. I heard you and my doctor talking outside. Was it about me or some other patient? Of course, I don't suppose you are allowed to talk about your patients, but can't you make an exception this once? I'm getting bored from inactivity."

34

"Be thankful you are getting well, my dear," Kathy said, her gray eyes clouded. "My present patient is a young engineer. His right hand was crushed, and there is talk of amputation. He is frantic with worry, and so is his family. I hope we can save his hand. I am not at all sure that amputation is imperative. I have seen much worse cases than his, in fact one of them was my own brother, but the only one who gives me the least bit of encouragement is Dr. Elliott, the senior intern, but of course he can't go against Dr. Blaine."

"Do you know, Nurse?" Dana said softly. "I don't like Dr. Blaine and neither does my grandmother, though for different reasons, I suspect. And I have a feeling that he and my doctor, Dr. MacDonald, have no especial love for each other either, although no one has said anything, of course. Do you like him—the Chief, I mean?"

Kathy laughed into the serious brown eyes of the girl in the narrow bed. "He's my Chief, Dana," she told her evasively, "and I have no reason—no personal reason—for disliking him. He is a fine surgeon, but very austere and almost harsh with the nurses who work with him. I always dread being assigned to the O.R. when he's operating, although his work is wonderful, almost miraculous. But I guess we are all pretty scared of him."

"Well, I'm not scared of him," Dana Adams boasted. "I don't like him. What business is it of his if I have company? I like company and I'm not sick. My friends are never noisy or annoying, but we do have good times when they come to see me. Maybe that's it. Maybe he's a misanthropist and hates everyone. I'm glad he wasn't here when I came a cropper. I haven't any patience with such people. After all, the world is a pretty fine place, and the people are pretty decent, too."

She laughed, a brief tinkling chime of bells, and went on.

"That reminds me. Gram has a friend who is a famous novelist. He writes constantly and makes a great deal of money. But I don't like some of his books, and once when he was visiting us I asked him point-blank, as uninhibited teen-agers will on occasion—I had no least intention of being rude, you know, but it had been troubling me for some time—and I said, 'Mr. Brandon, why don't some of you famous authors write about good people? After all, there are more good people in the world than there are the other kind.' And do you know what he answered? I think it was a terrible commentary on America's literary taste. He said, 'I know, my dear, but no one wants to read about them.' No doubt he was right, because we have only to watch the sales of a risqué novel mount to know it is true. But that is beside the point. We were talking about your Chief. Do you know, Kathy—I shall call you Kathy; it's more personal, and I like you very much."

"I'm glad you do, Dana," the nurse replied, "because I like you, too."

"I was going to say that I actually cringe when your Chief comes into this room, and yet I'm not in the least afraid of him. It's just that I don't like him. Who does he think he is, anyway? What if he is a great surgeon? What if most of his operations are successful? It should make him humble and very grateful for his God-given ability, instead of the reverse—arrogant and harsh with his associates. I hope you save that poor fellow's hand, Kathy. I wish my doctor was on the case. Dr. MacDonald is wonderful."

She was startled at the sudden flush that spread over the other's lovely face from throat to hairline. But before she could say anything more the young nurse made a hasty retreat, leaving the girl in the hospital bed puzzled and a bit perturbed. And yet why not? What could be more understandable than that Dr. MacDonald should fall in love with Kathy Marshall? She was so sweet, but just the same Dana Adams didn't like the idea one bit.

The entrance of her grandmother dispelled the sudden gloom that had settled on the girl's spirits. The strange part of it was that she had no idea of the reason for it.

"Have you been in to see Dana Adams lately, Barker?" Kathy Marshall asked her friend that same afternoon, as the two met in the gymnasium.

"Not lately or at all, Kathy," the other replied. "Why?"

"Do you mean to say that you haven't met her?"

The older nurse shook her head. "Why should I? Just who is she that I should make the effort?"

"Oh, she's a very attractive girl and—well, most of the nurses, and doctors too, are quite enamored of her. She's sweet—charming would be a better word, I suppose—and she is making rapid progress toward complete recovery. She broke her hip last October, you know, while I was in

Receiving. And you haven't been in to see her? Hasn't Dr. Channing suggested it?"

Irene Barker swung around and stared at the younger girl. "Just what do you mean by that question?"

"Nothing, only I heard him say it was a pity more patients weren't like her. It seems the nurses report that a visit with her is like a shot in the arm. I like her a lot. She's young, unspoiled, and much attracted to her doctor."

"And who is her doctor?"

"Gary MacDonald," Kathy replied demurely. "You should listen to her ravings."

"And how about him? That's the point I'm interested in."

"Of course he's fond of her. He couldn't help it."

"Huh!" the older nurse muttered. "Well, I hope it's true."

Kathy Marshall said nothing. She felt sure she was not the least bit in love with Dr. MacDonald. She liked and admired him very much indeed, and she felt sure that he liked her, but—well there was no room in her plans for men, doctors or otherwise. She meant to make a career of nursing. She felt sure it was her calling. She knew she was a good nurse. She liked her job and found the arduous work satisfying, and although there were times when she wondered if her efforts were appreciated—when a patient was uncooperative, querulous, and impossible to please—she had come to realize that if the situation were reversed and she was in the patient's place she might be even worse. And so she went on her even course, cheerful, uncomplaining, meeting each new problem in stride, acquiring the reputation of being an ideal nurse. Nearly always this plain, common-sense reasoning was all that she needed to dispel any dissatisfaction or restlessness that might for the moment irk her.

She had been on the Latham case for several nights now and wondered why the Chief continued to postpone the amputation about which he had spoken so emphatically. Was it possible that the great Dr. Blaine was in doubt? Of course not. He was famous for his quick diagnoses—and seldom changed his original decision. That fact worried Kathy, and it worried the Latham family, too.

All during the days and nights of delirium, the patient cried out against amputation, constantly demanding a

37

promise from his brother, wife, nurse, and doctor to let him die instead. So it was that, when word reached them by the ever-active grapevine that the Chief had been suddenly called away on an important medical matter, both nurse and doctor breathed a sigh of relief. Bob Latham's hand appeared to be healing very well. Dr. Elliott watched it closely, and he and Kathy silently congratulated each other every time they met in the Latham room. Indeed, Bill Elliott had come across similar and even worse cases during the war.

Young Jim Latham, Bob's younger brother, dropped in on the evening following the Chief's departure with the news that Dr. Scott from Boston was coming to take a look at his brother's hand that same night.

"He should be here any minue now," he told them jubilantly. "I'm frank to tell you that he hesitated, but I happen to know his son Doug—we were in Yale together one year—and so he consented on condition that Blaine had no objections. I wired him that Blaine happened to be out of town and that no one need know of his visit. Of course, he discounted that angle but—well, he's coming."

He turned and left the room and returned in a few minutes with a tall, pleasant-faced man who shook hands with Dr. Elliott, smiled paternally at the nurse, and moved over to the bed.

"So you're the great Bob Latham?" he asked jovially. "Do you know, young man, I've been pretty well fed up with you and your prowess. Doug has talked of little else since that last engineering feat of yours."

All the time he was talking he was examining the injured hand. At last he turned to Dr. Elliott.

"This looks to be all right. No least sign of infection here. Tell me, Doctor, just why—no, I shall not ask that. Sometimes I come across much the same conditions down East. You have a fine man here, Doctor. I should like to meet him again. I think I met him at one of our national conventions, but I doubt if he would recall the occasion."

To the patient, he said pleasantly, "I doubt if you should be hospitalized much longer. That hand will never be as strong as it was before—you'll just have to do a bit of training of your left. Oh, you'll be able to use it, but the palm or metacarpus has been injured to the extent of lessening the efficiency of the fingers. I'm sure you will still find it useful in many ways, but I should advise caution. Let your brain serve you for a while, my boy, and take a long rest. You're nervous, keyed up, perhaps even worried. Let Mother Nature get to work on you, Bob, and you'll be surprised how different life will look."

He turned again to Dr. Elliott.

"Give my regards to Dr. Blaine, Doctor, and tell him I was sorry to miss him. Goodbye, Bob. Jim, suppose you accompany me to the station. Doug gave me enough messages to exhaust a far more indulgent parent than I, but I shall do my best to relay them. The boy misses you, I suspect."

"Aren't you flying back, Doctor?" Jim asked, knowing he had arrived by plane.

The great man shook his head. "No," he answered, "I have sleeping accommodations on a train due in twenty minutes. Let's go. A cab is waiting." He shook hands again with the doctor, smiled at patient and nurse, lifted a hand in parting salute, and was gone.

"Well," Dr. Elliott murmured as the door closed. "That was certainly a hasty call, but do you know, Marshall? In spite of the storm I feel sure his visit is going to stir up, I'm relieved to have his opinion, although it confirmed my own. I wonder——" He paused, and his grin told Kathy more than any words he could have said.

"I'm still here, Doctor," the patient told them, and his voice and face were those of a different person. Gone were the haggard lines and the frightened eyes. Instead there were optimism and a buoyancy that had been absent during the days of his hospitalization. "How soon do you think I can go home? I should like to get out of here before Dr. Blaine gets back."

"No, you don't, my fine fellow." Dr. Elliott grinned down at him. "We need Exhibit A. We need to show the Chief what a job your nurse and I have done in saving that hand of yours for you—and for humanity, I might say. I don't think the Chief will blow his top—unethical, you know. I'll be the fall guy, and I might even be kicked out, but my year of internship is nearly over anyway."

"Oh, they won't let you go, Dr. Elliott," Kathy told him. "You have done wonderful work since you have been here, and we all know it, even Dr. Blaine. I know he has mentioned it to several people. Anyway, I'm in this too, you know. I, too, objected to amputation."

The young doctor's eyes were tender as he surveyed the lovely girl beside him. "I should be able to stand anything if you're with me, Marshall—Kathy," he murmured, his hands on her shoulders.

"Sure," Bob Latham added. "I'm not looking, Doctor, but you're dead right. Go on and kiss her if you want to. I'm a married man or I would myself."

"Don't be silly," Kathy said severely, although her face was rosy and her heart threatened to choke her. For a moment Dr. Elliott looked as if he meant to take Bob Latham's advice, but the opening of the door, admitting Jim Latham, eased the situation.

CHAPTER FIVE

JUST WHAT'S ALL THE EXCITEMENT about, Marshall?" Irene Barker asked, when she stopped in at Kathy's room one afternoon. "Liz Morton told me the Chief was giving Elliott skates about something or other. She couldn't get the details, but she did hear Dr. Elliott tell his nibs that he was quite ready to leave the hospital at any time, but that he saw no reason for Dr. Blaine to be incensed at what was a perfectly natural act on the part of a patient's relatives, especially in the absence of the Chief himself. I have a notion that last statement was a clincher and one the boss couldn't refute. What do you know about it, Kathy?"

But the younger nurse shook her head. She had no desire to discuss the situation that would probably cost Bill Elliott his place on the staff. To be sure, his year of internship was nearly over, but he had intended staying on for a few months in order to work directly under Dr. Blaine before taking over a practice of his own. Kathy hated gossip and tried to keep away from anything remotely resembling it.

But the older nurse scoffed. "You've been Bob Latham's night nurse ever since he came here, and I heard Bill Elliott tell Channing that you also refused to believe that amputation was the only thing that would save the man's life. Didn't he make his wife and brother promise never to let them amputate? I heard that he did, and that during those first days and nights of delirium that was his whole cry. So don't tell me you know nothing about it, or about a certain Dr. Scott making a brief visit one night while the Chief was absent. Things like that can't be kept hidden, you know, so you might as well come clean. I'm no gossip, but I do like to keep abreast of what is going on in this place. So give, darling, and you need have no fear it will go farther."

"Is Dr. Elliott really leaving, Irene?" Kathy wanted to know.

Irene Barker shook her head. "The Chief won't let him go, Kathy. And do you know, I have an idea that the Chief has begun to realize that his own job here isn't nearly as solid as it used to be, or as he thought it was. Elliott stands well with the Board, and with Bostwick in general. I doubt if the Chief will let him go. But he was plenty burned up, from all reports. Now tell me just what happened, Kathy. You might as well, for I'll hear a garbled account of it from others."

Kathy reluctantly told her friend the story of Dr. Scott's hasty visit.

"And he approved of the treatment we had given the patient, urged him to take it easy, and told him he could leave the hospital in a week or so," she finished.

"And how about the hand, Kathy? Will it be all right?"

"He only said it would never be as strong as before, and advised training the left hand. Bob Latham is going home this afternoon." She bit her lip and frowned for a moment. "Do you know, Irene, I don't think this affair has added anything to the Chief's popularity here in Bostwick, Jim Latham hinted that he had been steadily losing prestige for some time. Have you heard anything about that?"

Irene Barker grinned at her friend. "Only gossip, darling, and you don't approve of gossip. But seriously, Kathy," she went on, "it has been a wonder to me, for several years now, why people stand for his arrogance and harshness. Let me tell you something that happened to a friend of mine just this last fall. Her husband had to have one of his kidneys removed. He was pretty sick. He's a comparatively young man; his wife is only a few years older than I am. Just an average couple—not at all wealthy, but managing to get along. He was here in Memorial for several weeks, and after he returned home he was in bed for some time."

She paused. "One night—it must have been after midnight when things always look blackest—he complained of nausea and intense pain in his side, so his wife called Dr. Blaine, the man who had operated on her husband. She

41

wanted reassurance, more than anything else, and naturally went to the man who she felt might give it. But instead he told her that her husband was no longer a patient of his— he was a surgeon, not a physician—and not to disturb him again. The poor woman was completely flabbergasted until her husband advised calling the family doctor. She did so, and he came immediately, and his very presence was all that was needed to help them both. Of course that story lost nothing in the repeating, and the Chief lost more of his phony glamor—the glamor that has surrounded him for years. No, Kathy, I don't think the Chief is at all popular with Bostwickians, unless, of course, they are in need of serious operations. Then, I'll grant you, he's good —none better—but that diabolical disposition will be his ruin yet."

"It's too bad," the younger nurse murmured. "I can't say I really like the Chief, although I do admire his ability."

"That's the way I feel," her friend agreed. "But his over-bearing, contemptuous attitude toward members of the staff is slowly undermining the morale of the place. Even Ann Merriman senses it, and she has been one of Blaine's stanchest admirers ever since she became Superintendent here. As it is, she has become something of a buffer between the Chief and members—male members, especially—of the staff. I don't know how long it is going to last, because I heard him reprimand Annie just the other day; and, while she took it and said nothing in reply, I found her pacing her office later, her face aflame. I drew my own conclusions. Ann Merriman is ace-high with the staff and the town in general, and I think it's only her love for Memorial and her desire to keep things running smoothly that she stands him at all. I doubt if I would."

"Was he always like this, Irene?" Kathy asked.

"Apparently not, or he would never have reached his present place in the sun. No, my own opinion is that his failure to get something he wanted has eaten like a canker into his heart—or what passes for his heart. Can this be love, Kathy?"

Kathy Marshall shook her head. "Nearer hate, Irene," she answered. "Hate does that to people, I'm told. Poor Dr. Blaine! Do you know, I feel very sorry for him. He's so clever, such a marvelous surgeon—oh, I don't know. I wish I could do something to help him."

42

Irene Barker laughed scornfully. "Save your pity and your altruistic schemes, my dear. The great Blaine asks nothing of anyone. My advice is to leave him strictly alone."

"I probably shall," the other answered, and opened the door to let the older nurse precede her from the room.

Kathy was to have the night off duty and before dinner she stopped in at room 407 for a chat with Dana Adams.

"I want to go home for Christmas, Kathy," the girl in the narrow hospital bed cried. "My own doctor thinks it would be all right. I have been up in a chair now several times since the casts came off, and I don't see why I have to stay here any longer. Pete will be home for the holidays, and with Butch there and Gram and Nick Dalton, who has promised to come in every day to help me learn to walk, I can't see any sense in my staying on here running up bills. Heaven knows they're high enough already. But no, Dr. Blaine thinks it most unwise for me to leave the hospital for at least another two weeks, and he insists that I try using a walker."

Angry tears filled the brown eyes of the girl and she dashed an impatient hand across them.

"I told him right out that I wouldn't use the walker, and he glared at me and informed me that the nurses here in the hospital were far too busy to teach me to walk. I told him I had plenty of volunteers to help me, and I didn't need the nurses. While we were raving at each other Dr. MacDonald arrived and calmed the troubled waters, as far as I was concerned. He patted my shoulder and told me to take it easy, that everything would work out all right, and that a few days more in the hospital wouldn't hurt me and would give Gram and Butch time to perfect certain plans they were making. The big boss ignored him completely, but before he left the room he said, 'I have made arrangements to have a walker delivered to your room at three this afternoon, Miss Adams. I shall expect you to use it.'"

"And what did your doctor say to that, Dana?" Kathy was interested to learn.

"Oh, he merely replied that a walker was not at all necessary under the circumstances."

"And the Chief? What was his reply?"

"He didn't even pause, but repeated that the walker would be here at three and he expected me to try using it."

"And did it and did you?"

"No. I threw a fit, Kathy." The girl grinned through her tears. "I never did such a thing in my life before, but I scared the nurses half to death. I guess they thought I had lost my wits, but just then Butch arrived and did he speak his mind! He informed those nurses that we were paying for this room, and that while I was in it there was to be no more unpleasantness or disturbance. I was proud of my kid brother, Kathy. Butch shoved that walker out into the corridor and invited the nurses to follow it." The girl wiped her wet eyes and grinned, even though Kathy was sure she felt more like crying.

"And are you going home for Christmas, Dana?" the nurse asked.

"My doctor says I am, but what authority has he, Kathy? Can he go over the Chief's head? Will it make trouble for him if he does? I don't want that, but oh, I want to be home for Christmas! I do! I do!" Tears came again, and Kathy tried to quiet her. It was upon this scene that the Superintendent of Nurses arrived.

"Just what is wrong, my dear?" she asked gently. "Don't you like us here? Haven't we been kind to you that you are so anxious to leave us?"

"It—it isn't that, Miss Merriman," Dana whimpered. "It's that it won't be Christmas if I'm not home with my family. They count on it, and so do I, and I can't see why——"

"Sometimes we can't understand certain disappointments, child," the Superintendent told her. "After all, this is a hospital, you know, and Dr. Blaine is a very wonderful surgeon and probably feels that so much excitement would not be beneficial to you. Won't you try to understand? I'm sure your own doctor, Dr. MacDonald, has come to agree with our Chief in this. After all, it won't be long until you can go home, able to walk and dance to your heart's content. You have made a wonderful recovery, my dear, and we here in Memorial are proud of you."

Dana had quieted down. She listened silently to the Superintendent's words, and Kathy watched her closely to see if she had become at all reconciled to remaining hospitalized through the holidays. At last, Miss Merriman rose and patted the girl's cheek. Kathy smiled as the older woman went quietly from the room.

"I suppose you think I'm just a big baby, don't you, Kathy?" she muttered. "I suppose I am, too, but—oh, I guess I can stand a couple more weeks here. But," she added, her mouth stubborn, "I shall not use that darned walker, and no one is going to make me."

Kathy Marshall wondered, as she walked down the long corridor to the elevator and on to her room in the nurses' annex, just how she was going to manage. She wondered, too, just why the Chief was so insistent upon her remaining in the hospital for two or more weeks longer. The hospital was crowded, and yet he probably knew his business—or was it because Dr. MacDonald had said the girl could go home in time for the holidays?

There was a note from Irene Barker on the desk, saying she was not eating in the hospital but that she had eaten a quick lunch with an ex-patient and would see her later. So Kathy went down to dinner alone, and somehow she discovered she wasn't hungry. She missed her friend and the sprightly talk Irene always had at her tongue's end. But she lingered at the table, entering into the discussion of some half dozen girls eager and excited over Christmas preparations. And it was some time later that she pulled her cape closely about her and stepped out into the open side porch.

The early December dark had already descended. It was bitterly cold, one of those silent white nights when snow seemed to muffle all sound. Kathy's breath came in little puffs of steam. She wondered whether to ask Irene to go to a movie with her, or if it would be better to spend this rare night off resting in her room with a book or a new magazine.

Inside, the maid met her at the foot of the stairs with the announcement that there was a call for her. Dr. Elliott wanted her to call him at the Center as soon as she came in. Kathy wondered what he wanted and moved over to the small telephone closet to put through the call.

"You're off duty tonight?" he asked, and as she answered that she was he went on, "So am I. Would you like to go for a real honest-to-goodness sleigh ride—horse and cutter, buffalo robe, bells, and all the rest of it? There's a moon tonight, and millions of stars are scheduled, and—"

Kathy gasped. "But how about the rules, Doctor?" she wanted to know. "Have you forgotten?"

She heard a light laugh at the other end of the line, and then the man said, "I've taken care of everything, Kathy. Annie knows about it and has promised to hear no evil, see no evil, and speak no evil. Put on your warmest clothes and come on. I'll meet you just outside the door of your cloister in one half hour. O.K.?"

"I'll be ready, Doctor," she laughed. "It will be fun."

"I'm Bill to you, Kathy," the man said softly, as he hung up.

The girl ran up the stairs to her room, where she found Irene Barker just entering.

"What's the excitement, Marshall?" the older nurse asked. "Has someone left you a fortune? There are stars in your eyes and——"

"I'm going for a sleigh ride, Irene!" Kathy cried ecstatically. "Imagine! Isn't that precious?"

"Sleigh ride?" the other said doubtfully. "Are you sure? And, if I may ask, who with?"

Kathy hesitated to answer. Then, with finger on lip, she replied as she reached in her closet for a warm woolen frock and sweater, "Dr. Elliott. Can you bear it, Irene? He just called me. And he got permission, too—and from no less a person than Annie herself."

"Good for Elliott!" Barker applauded. Then, suddenly sobering, "I hope the Chief doesn't get wind of it. But then," she added comfortingly, "he probably won't. You wear my new fur coat, Kathy. It's lots warmer than yours, and being a larger size you can wrap it snugly around your legs."

"Oh, Bill—Dr. Elliott—assured me there would be a robe in the sleigh. Isn't it wonderful, Irene? I haven't been on a sleigh ride since I came east. I'm thrilled to death. Oo la la! Isn't life wonderful?" And while her friend went across the hall for the new fur coat, Kathy dressed excitedly.

"Better wear a hood, or at least something to cover your ears, Kathy," Irene urged. "Cutters are open to the winds of heaven, as I remember them, and you don't want to risk frozen ears. It's nearly zero outside, but I suppose your youth and exuberance will keep you warm. I'm here to tell you, my dear, that I'm darned glad it's Bill Elliott instead of Gary MacDonald you're going with. That would be crowding your luck. The Chief would be sure to get wind of it,

and then—pouf! Off would go somebody's head. There!"
she exclaimed, as she tied the heavy veil over the younger
girl's ears and under her chin. "You look cute. Have a
grand time, darling, and I'll keep a lookout for your return and let you in. Off with you. I hear the bells. Jingle
bells—I haven't thought of them in years. Good luck. Have
a wonderful evening!"

Kathy hurried down the stairs and was helped by Dr.
Elliott into the sleigh and covered snugly with a robe. The
bells jingled, the horse seemed to feel a return of youth,
the stars shone, and the big round moon shed a pathway of
gold before them. Kathy found herself singing softly the
words of an old song they used to sing on sleigh rides
back home in Wisconsin. Soon she was joined by a rather
uncertain bass, and then they were laughing together. And
so by turns, singing and laughing and then companionably
quiet, they left Bostwick and sped out into the silent and
white countryside.

CHAPTER SIX

IN SPITE OF THE CHIEF'S harsh decision that Dana Adams
should remain hospitalized over the holidays, the days were
exciting and happy for the injured girl. Gifts poured in,
and on the morning before Christmas Butch managed
somehow to bring in a sizable and well-proportioned tree,
which he set up at the foot of his sister's bed.

"How did you manage it, Butch?" Dana asked, her eyes
big with excitement. "Didn't someone try to stop you?"

Butch shook his head and looked smug. "I watched my
chance and snuck it in when the woman at the desk wasn't
looking. Once in the elevator, it was easy. You know, the
floor nurse is a sort of pal of mine; she wouldn't object. I'm
going down to the car after the trimmings. Gram is bringing in some things, too. She's as excited as you are, Sis. Do
you know, there's something about Christmas——"

"Yes," a voice came from the doorway, "isn't there? So,
if you couldn't go to Christmas, you had Christmas brought
to you. Is that the idea?" The voice was grave although the
eyes were twinkling.

"It's all right, isn't it, Doctor?" Dana demanded. "After
all——"

"Sure it's all right, Doc," Butch asserted belligerently.
"It's still Dana's room, she's paying for it, and——"

"He's kidding, Butch," Dana said. "Look at his eyes. Maybe there will even be a present on it for you, Doctor," she told him. "Gram thinks you're wonderful."

"And the rest of the family?" he teased.

"Oh, you'll pass, Doc," Butch told him, slipping from the room.

Gary MacDonald smiled at the patient. "Great youngster, Butch," he told the boy's sister. "You're a lucky girl, Dana Adams."

"You don't have to tell me that, Doctor," the girl replied seriously. "And one of the luckiest things that ever happened to me was having you on hand to take care of me, instead of the great Dr. Blaine. I have a feeling that maybe I wouldn't be able to dance, ever again, if he had had the handling of that break. Somehow I don't think your famous Chief believes much in youth or in dancing or, for that matter, in Dana Adams. Not that I care what he thinks, as long as you are on the job, Doctor. But please don't ever turn me over to him, no matter what happens. Promise?"

The young surgeon looked startled for a moment. Then he asked quickly, "Just what do you mean, Dana? Turn you over to Dr. Blaine? Why should I? Is something wrong? Are you in pain? Tell me."

Dana smiled, although her eyes were wet. "No, no," she reiterated. "It's just that he has been so insistent that I remain here until after the holidays that I—well, I wondered if he knew something the rest of us didn't. About me, I mean."

Dr. MacDonald shook his head. "Don't be fanciful, my dear. There's not a thing wrong with you. Your chart gives you a clean bill of health, and it is merely a concession to the head of Bostwick Memorial that you are here now. . . . Oh, good morning, Mrs. Hammond." He looked behind her for Butch. "Didn't Butch come back with you?"

"Oh, the woman at the desk stopped him, and you know my grandson, Doctor. He dearly loves an argument. He'll no doubt be along in a minute or two. Did you want him for something?"

The doctor watched the old lady stoop over the bed and lift the girl into her arms, where she cuddled her against her shoulder for a moment before returning her to the pillows. "Doesn't she look well, Doctor?" she asked.

48

"Perfect," the young man agreed. "I believe the enforced rest has done her a world of good. Dana is inclined to drive herself, to burn the candle at both ends—oh, not in riotous living, of course," he hastened to add, "but in doing more than she should. After all, there are only twenty-four hours in a day, and at least eight of them should be spent in sleep. I have a notion our patient has many times forgotten that. Well, for a time, at least, her activities will be somewhat curtailed, and we must see that she doesn't overdo."

"Now you sound just like Dr. Blaine," Dana pouted. "Don't you realize that I'm young, healthy, and that I've lost nearly three precious months in this hospital?"

"She doesn't mean it, Doctor," Mrs. Hammond said soothingly, "never fear. We intend seeing to it that our girl lives a bit more moderately—for a time at least," she finished, as a small hoot of derision came from the girl.

Butch flung into the room. "Did you bring in everything, Gram?" he demanded, opening a suitcase full of tree ornaments. "Let's get busy. I want to get it done before a bunch of snoopers come in."

"I wish I might borrow you for a little while, Butch," Dr. MacDonald said. "There's someone over in Pediatrics I should like to have you meet."

"Pediatrics?" Butch asked doubtfully. "That's the children's ward, isn't it? Why should I go there, Doc? And who is it you want me to meet?"

"Run along, dear," Mrs. Hammond urged. "I'll go on with the work, and if you don't like my artistic efforts you can change things when you come back."

Butch looked dubious. "Don't let anyone push you around, Gram," he advised. "This is the darnedest place for giving advice—most of it unpleasant—that I ever saw. O.K., Doc, let's go. I'll be right back, sis."

"Now, just what did all that nonsense mean, Butch?" the doctor inquired, as they moved down the long corridor to the elevator. "Who would want—or dare—to push Mrs. Hammond around? I can't imagine anyone having the temerity to attempt it. And who has been giving you unpleasant advice?"

"Oh, it's a long story, Doc," the boy said. "Forget it. Just where is this ward for kids? I don't know much about this place, thank heaven! I detest hospitals."

49

Dr. MacDonald laughed. "Of course that last isn't true, and you know it. Hospitals are wonderful places. What should we do without them? What would your sister have done without the care and treatment she has received here in Memorial? No, Butch, while I can understand your not knowing much about hospitals, I'm very sure you don't detest them. Here we are," he said, opening a door. "I want you to meet a youngster who thinks you are Superman, the hero of Roger Bostwick High, and the idol of his boyish heart. So, my lad, be especially kind to my young friend in the last bed on the left. His name is Tony Salinski. He's eleven, a grand boy and brave as they come."

The young doctor was met with grins and cries of welcome as he passed down the long ward, and he had a word for everyone.

"Hello, there, Tony!" he greeted the grinning child in the narrow bed. "You see, your wish has been granted, and here is Butch Adams, the star of many a basketball game, and not only basketball but football as well." He laid an affectionate arm across the older boy's shoulder and added, "Butch is just as pleased to meet you, Tony, as you are to have him here. Sit down for a moment, Butch, while I visit a few of my patients here. Yes, Wilson?"

He turned to a hovering nurse. They moved on down the long ward, leaving the two boys together. "How is he, Nurse?" he asked quietly.

The nurse shook her head, her eyes sad. "He had a bad night, Doctor. For a time Martin feared he might lose his fight, and she was about ready to call you—or," she added somewhat grudgingly, "the Chief—but he rallied, and then Dr. Channing happened along and the boy became easier. But I feel that another attack like that will undoubtedly——"

"I know," the young man murmured. "If it were merely his spine, we might—but the two—his heart is permanently injured. We can't look for much in the way of improvement. I wish I could spend more time with him. He is putting up such a good fight. . . ."

The doctor's voice trailed off; he was talking more to himself than to the nurse. He turned to look back at the bed, beside which Butch Adams sat deep in a detailed account of that last hectic game. It was evidently football this time, and the thin youngster in the hospital bed was watching with rapt, adoring eyes.

"Do you think the excitement is good for him, Doctor?" the nurse asked, diffidently, because after all one didn't question anything a doctor did or suggested, although Dr. MacDonald was different from some of the others.

Gary MacDonald shook his head. "Nothing can really harm him now, Wilson," he told her sadly. "Let the child have what happiness he can obtain from seeing and talking with a boy who is the embodiment of all that his youthful heart hoped he, himself, would someday become. It won't be long, Nurse, and we will let him have this precious hour to take with him into the Great Beyond."

"Father Murphy gave him the last rites yesterday, Doctor," the nurse explained. "But I doubt if the child understood. I feel sure he was practically unconscious at the time. Somehow, Dr. MacDonald," she went on, "I can't see any reason for Tony's death. What purpose, what object, will have been gained? Sometimes I fear I must be something of an atheist, Doctor. The death of a child always affects me like that. I can't understand why. Why?"

The young doctor laid a comforting hand on her shoulder. "None of us can, Wilson," he told her. "I can only say, God's ways are not our ways and He knows best. So, 'Let not your heart be troubled, neither let it be afraid. . . .' Perhaps Butch has stayed long enough," he went on, "but I couldn't let the boy die without a glimpse of his hero."

He was surprised to see that Butch seemed almost as reluctant to leave as the sick boy was to see him go. Their hands clung for a long moment, and when the doctor drew near the bed he heard the visitor say, "Chin up, Tony. Everything's going to be all right. You'll see. I'll be in again, fella. Good-by."

"Gosh, Doc," he whispered, as the two left the ward. "Tony's going to check out, isn't he? I could feel it. He's slipping already. Is that why you wanted me to come here?"

"That's the reason, Butch," the doctor told him. "Tony has talked of little else since reading of your athletic prowess and has wished so very much that he could see you in person. I think he will slip away some time this afternoon or tonight, Butch, and I aim to be with him. He's a fighter after my own heart."

"Just what was it? What happened to him?" Butch wanted to know, as they entered the elevator in the main building and pushed the button for the fourth floor. Somehow the trimming of a Christmas tree seemed trivial indeed. Almost he wished he hadn't brought it, hadn't tried to bring gaiety and laughter into this house of pain and death.

"Truck accident," the doctor told him tersely. "His parents were both killed at the time. Tony's spine was hopelessly twisted, and his heart, evidently never strong, was permanently injured. We have tried everything we know here at Memorial to help him. You know, of course, that Dr. Blaine is one of the best surgeons in the country, at least that is his rating, but the case proved hopeless from the start. I feel, Butch, that the going when it comes will be quick. His vitality is low, as is his resistance. But I'm glad he had a chance to see you. Thank you for coming, for being such a good sport."

"Don't thank me, Doc, and don't call me a good sport," Butch said quickly. "It's Tony who's the good sport. I wish I could do something for him, something really worth-while. How about taking Dana's Christmas tree down there, presents and everything? She wouldn't mind, if she knew."

The doctor shook his head. "I'm afraid it would be useless, Butch," he murmured, 'and I'm sure the Chief would object. He insists upon complete quiet and urged that a screen be placed around the boy's bed to insure privacy. However, I have fought that. Tony is essentially a friendly youngster. He likes visiting with the others, and until the very last that screen is going to remain against the wall where I placed it this morning. I've left word in my office that I'm not available unless absolutely needed, and the rest of my day and evening is going to be spent in Pediatrics, Butch, where I can watch and help and maybe pray that brave young Tony Salinski may have a safe and painless journey across into that Other Country. Out you go, Butch, and thank you for helping. Have a grand time trimming Dana's tree, and I'll try to drop in before you leave this evening." He grinned at the serious-faced young man beside him. "Of course you'll be here this evening—Christmas Eve?"

Butch's face lightened. "What do you think, Doc?" He sent his companion an answering grin, and the two parted.

Butch strove desperately to shake off the experience through which he had just passed, as he walked slowly down the long corridor to his sister's room. A nurse stopped him.

"Tell me," she asked inquisitively, an impish look on her pretty face, "how on earth did you manage to get that huge tree past the dragon downstairs and into 407? Why, I attempted to take a teeny-weeny one up to my room in the annex and was promptly hauled over the coals for being childish and rebellious. Imagine! And it wasn't in this old hospital at all, but in my own dreary little room on the top floor of the annex. Sometimes this place gets my goat, Butch, do you know that? Sometimes I'm tempted to quit and study stenography—only I'm not so hot in spelling."

Butch laughed. "Oh, stick to nursing, Kate," he urged. "You're over the hump. The rest won't be so bad, and think nothing of that Christmas tree stunt. I just used the old bean, that's all. Stop in and give it the once-over before you hole up for the night. Maybe Santa Claus has left you a gift. One can never tell, you know. See you later."

During the months of his sister's hospitalization, Butch had become a pal and advocate of every nurse in Bostwick Memorial. He called every one of them, even the older women, by their first names and they loved it. He grinned companionably at doctors and interns, and even the Chief himself was not entirely immune to the infectious grin with which the boy met his dour greeting if and when the doctor deigned to notice him at all. He was popular with the entire staff, and he knew it and sometimes took advantage of that popularity to ignore visiting hours and to make infringements on rules and customs sacred to the old institution. Dana used to tell him that he would get into trouble, but he pooh-poohed the idea and continued to enjoy his sister's incarceration.

And this Christmas was no exception. The trimming of the tree soon filled his heart and mind so that his experience of the morning faded and at last disappeared altogether. Nurses dropped in at 407 to admire the tree and to receive some small gift from Gram or the redoubtable Butch. Even when Peter arrived, in the afternoon,

53

accompanied by Dr. Blaine himself, the holiday atmosphere continued unabated.

"Humph!" the Chief muttered, his austere gaze on the glowing tree at the foot of the bed. "Christmas! I suppose you still believe in Santa Claus?" he said harshly.

"Of course," Dana replied promptly. "And to prove it here is a small gift that he left on the tree for you. Hand it to him, Gram. There!" she continued. "Your very first Christmas gift. Open it!" she demanded. "Open it! Aren't you thrilled?"

"Thrilled?" he retorted, still harshly. "And why should I be thrilled at something—a joke, no doubt—provided by someone with a perverted sense of humor?" He tossed it unopened on the bed and turned quickly as a trio of nurses appeared. "What is this?" he barked. "Have you nothing to do? This is a hospital, not a social club. I never heard of such behavior! Leave at once, all of you!"

"But—but, Dr. Blaine!" Dana cried unhappily. "You have left your gift, and it is a nice gift—especially for you. Please take it." She reached down to the foot of the bed and retrieved the small, gaily wrapped package, and Butch practically forced it on him.

"Don't be such a spoilsport, Chief," he jibed derisively. "It's all in fun and in the spirit of Christmas. Come on, Doctor, have a bite of Gram's really super Christmas cake —made according to a recipe handed down from the daughter of Pharaoh to Gram herself. One bite and you're lost. The old man passeth and the new man is born. Here, I'll be generous, Doctor. Come in, girls, and see the Chief reborn." He stopped for a brief moment while the others held their collective breaths; and the Chief, with an effort that undoubtedly cost him much, received the fruit cake and took a nibble while Gram, her keen eyes twinkling, watched him.

All at once the room seemed rather crowded, and suddenly the Chief strode to the door. "I don't approve of this hilarity in a hospital," he growled. "Miss Adams, I reverse my decision. You are free to return home any time you wish, and the results be upon you and your personal physician's heads." He went out, and if it had been possible to slam the door he would no doubt have done so, only hospital doors don't slam.

The nurses looked scared, and Mrs. Hammond's face

54

showed dismay, but Butch struck an attitude. "Ladies and gentlemen," he began, then changed to, "Nurses, callers, and patients! You have just witnessed the transformation of a tyrant into a simple, disgruntled, small boy whom, once upon a time, Santa Claus forgot. Did he take his gift, Sis?" he asked. At her nod, he went on, "And from now on he can never again refuse to believe in the Christmas Saint because the gaily wrapped parcel contained a reasonable facsimile of Kris Kringle himself who possesses the power to hex or make believers of the most skeptical. So, my friends, from now on you are to treat your Chief of Staff as an equal, never as a superior. He is one of you and one with you. Farewell! Grab your gifts and beat it. We have work to do. Send the next batch in, Pete," he admonished his brother.

It was a gala occasion, and when later in the evening a saddened Gary MacDonald left the deathbed of Tony Salinski to enter the bright and happy 407, he was greeted by subdued cries of welcome as the others crowded around him.

"Dana's going home tonight, Doc," Butch told him above the others. "The Chief himself had a sudden change of heart and said so. That's the Christmas spirit for you! Come and get your present, Doc. Gram will hand it to you, and then we want to move this tree down to Pediatrics for the kids. There are quite a few things left on it and candy and popcorn for all. Can do, Doc?" he asked somewhat belatedly, as he sensed the young doctor's sober demeanor. "Oh!" he breathed. "It's too late. Never mind, Doc. Let's put it in the hall outside and give the nurses a thrill!"

"What is it?" Dana asked softly, as the doctor came to stand beside her bed.

But he shook his head. It was better not to mar the happiness that shone in the girl's eyes at the thought of spending Christmas at home after all. No, Tony had left his battered and suffering body for an indestructible one and would spend Christmas in the Eternal City.

"Has the ambulance been called, Mrs. Hammond?" he asked. No one had thought of that, so Dr. MacDonald put through a call for the ambulance, and everyone helped pack Dana's belongings into the big suitcase Butch had brought the decorations in. At a little after seven the stretcher arrived, and Dana left the hospital with a glowing heart. The elevator wouldn't hold all who were there, so some ran down the stairs and waited at the service entrance to speed her on her way.

"Good-by!" she called, above the bundling blanket that wrapped her like a mummy. "You have all been grand to me, and I hope you will come see me, every one of you."

Peter and Dr. MacDonald climbed in beside her, and the door was shut. Butch helped his grandmother into the family car and sped away, determined to reach home before the others should arrive. He did, and the house glowed with light as Dana was carried up the steps, through the wide hall, and into the bright living room. It was then the tears came.

Butch stared, appalled. "But why, Sis?" he demanded. "I thought you wanted to come home."

"Don't be such a dope!" his brother said inelegantly. "Of course she did. All girls cry when they're happy."

"Oh, yeah?" Butch retorted.

Gram said nothing for a moment but drew the girl into her arms and let her cry, while Dr. MacDonald nodded understandingly.

CHAPTER SEVEN

CHRISTMAS WAS OVER, and once again Bostwick Memorial Hospital had settled down to its usual uninspired routine. Somehow this last Christmas had been more hectic and more hilarious than any previous ones the staff could remember. Perhaps it was the influence of Butch Adams or perhaps it was the lessening of the stern requirements, the almost imperceptible softening of the Chief's demands. The staff was quick to notice, and the atmosphere of quiet happiness seemed to pervade the huge institution. The patients reflected it. The nurses responded to their calls for service more quickly and with much less irritation—inward and unvoiced, of course—and criticism. But then, the patients didn't seem so unreasonable in their demands; they were suddenly both cooperative and appreciative.

"Some leavening agency has been at work here, Marshall," Irene Barker mused aloud to her friend, as they strolled down the long hill to the drugstore at the foot. "Even the Chief appears to have absorbed a bit of the Yuletide spirit—not very much, understand, but a morsel of it. He actually greeted me—first, mind you—with a civil "good morning" when I ran into him at seven this morning while leaving the men's ward. I almost forgot to answer, I was so flabbergasted."

Kathy Marshall nodded. "I've noticed it too, Barker," she murmured. "And did you know he allowed Dana Adams to go home for the holidays after all? I believe his change of heart established something of a record here. Dr. Elliott told me that in the year he had been in Memorial he had never known such a thing to happen. Your friend, Dr. Channing, mentioned it, too. I wonder just what happened to him. Something, that's certain."

"Listen, Kathy." Irene stopped on the snowy street and spoke somewhat crossly, while her face showed more color than usual. "Stop calling Channing my friend."

"But isn't he, Irene?" the other inquired demurely.

"No more than he's yours and you know it. How would you like to have me call Bill Elliott your friend?"

"But, Irene," Kathy said quickly, "I hope he is my friend. I like him. He's kind and gentle and—I like him."

"O.K.," the older nurse told her, "so you like him. So he is your friend. But Dr. Elliott is quite different from Channing, Kathy. He's young, he's on the make, he's independent, and he shows you plainly that he likes you. Now on the other hand, Channing is Blaine's man. Afraid of his job. Doesn't dare risk offending the Chief even though he might know the big boss is wrong. And then, too, he's much a stickler for rules. Imagine Bob Channing daring to ask me for a date." Her tone was bitter, and Kathy was astonished. She had never thought of the popular Resident in that light.

"Oh, Irene!" she chided. "I think you're wrong. You never give him the least bit of encouragement. You're stiff and cool when he's around. I've noticed it. And he doesn't always agree with the Chief either. Remember Bob Latham's hand? He backed both Dr. Elliott and me to the very end, until Bob left the hospital. I think you're wrong in your estimate—if it is your honest estimate—of the Resident. I feel sure he admires you, but, darling," she went on gently, "you can be extremely difficult at times. A sort of 'keep your distance, Doctor, I don't fall for any of your blandishments' attitude."

Irene Barker laughed, although there was a break in her voice. "Do I really act like that, Kathy?" she asked. "I'm sure I never intended to. But doctors are a conceited lot, you know. They have an idea that any girl—nurse in particular—is theirs for the taking and should feel honored yielding to their overtures. I'm thirty-four, my dear, and that has been my experience."

Kathy shook the arm nearest her and said sternly, "You're misanthropic, Irene Barker. Just because you were hurt once—just because you happened to become mixed up with a cad, a contemptible rapscallion—is no reason for you to class all men in that category. Listen, Irene, you're letting it spoil your life. You're young, lovely, and desirable—and one of the best, if not the best, nurse in Memorial. I could shake you, only you're bigger than I am and we're still on the street and it's too cold. Let's have something hot to drink. I'll treat. Come on in."

The two entered the warm and crowded drugstore and found a small table for two. "I believe I'm hungry, Kathy," the older nurse said, almost apologetically. "And look at the dinner I disposed of. I could lose ten pounds to advantage, but just the same I shall have a chicken sandwich and a cup of coffee—black, I'm forced to say, although I love the trimmings." Kathy gave her order for the same, and the two settled down to enjoy themselves.

"We somehow got off the track back there," Kathy murmured as she gazed around the crowded room. "I have an idea we can thank Dana Adams and her family for the change in the atmosphere of the hospital, Irene. She's one of the nicest girls I have ever met, and her grandmother is all one could wish. I like her young brothers, too, although I don't know the older one very well. His name is Peter. He's attractive and made quite a hit among the girls here. Butch is a sketch. What that boy doesn't think of isn't worth doing. Why even Miss Merriman fell in love with him. Did he address you by your first name, Irene?" She grinned.

"Oh, yes," the other nodded, "but I imagine my manner dashed his high spirits a bit. He sort of avoided me later, although I liked the boy and might easily have fallen for his winning ways."

"And Dana?" Kathy prodded. "Didn't you fall in love with her as the rest of the staff did?"

Irene Barker shook her head. "Even Gary MacDonald, Kathy?" she asked, eyeing the younger girl warily.

Kathy's lovely face flushed as it always did at the mention of Gary MacDonald's name, but she nodded, trying hard to keep her voice cool. "I believe he did, Irene," she answered. "He was certainly devoted to her, and I'm sure she adores him. He's a fine man, Irene, and any girl should be proud to gain his love. Oh, oh, that looks good," she murmured, as the waitress approached with a tray. She was glad to change the subject.

"I doubt if it has come to that yet, Kathy," Irene Barker told her, making a wry face as she sipped her hot coffee. Then she added, "Speak of angels or the opposite and they're sure to appear. Here comes our Resident."

Kathy turned to smile up at the tall man approaching their table. He was eyeing the older nurse somewhat dubiously, and Kathy said, "We were just discussing you, Dr. Channing—oh, in just a general way," she added, her gaze shifting for a moment to her friend across the table.

"Are you among those who enjoy panning the opposite sex, Marshall?" the Resident asked, reaching a long foot to a vacant chair behind him and bringing it to the table. "I know I've suffered long from their armed barbs." His keen gaze probed the other girl, and Irene's face flamed for a moment then became unnaturally white.

"I hope you weren't being personal, Dr. Channing," Kathy reproved. "Neither of us enjoys panning anyone, least of all one we both admire as much as we do our Resident." She dimpled roguishly, her eyes on her plate.

"I somehow detect a note of derision in that remark, Marshall," he retorted, his gaze on the older nurse, who had recovered her poise.

"Don't be so suspicious, Dr. Channing," Kathy scolded. She kicked her friend sharply in the shin. "Oh, I nearly forgot to get my tooth paste. Please excuse me for a moment." She left the table and was annoyed to see the quick frown on Irene's face. Was Irene going to be distant and unfriendly again?

Kathy remained away from the table as long as she dared. She bought tooth paste she didn't need at the moment, dusting powder the clerk assured her was especially good, bath salts of which she was well supplied, and a magazine which she had already skimmed through that very afternoon. At last she strolled back to her friend, only to find that the Resident had departed, leaving Irene alone over her second cup of black coffee.

"Foiled again," was Irene's greeting, as Kathy piled her purchases on the vacant chair. "Tell me what you expected to gain by that obvious maneuver?"

"Gain? Maneuver? What maneuver?" Kathy asked innocently. "And what has become of Dr. Channing? Didn't he eat anything? Not even drink anything either? What on earth did you do to him, Irene? He seemed friendly enough when I left."

"Your leaving scared him away, Kathy," the older nurse told her. "The man's afraid of me." She bit her lip. "I'm a mess, Marshall," she muttered.

"You're nothing of the sort," Kathy contradicted stanchly. "I'm disappointed in Bob Channing. Is he a man or a mouse?"

"Sometimes one, sometimes the other, Marshall," the Resident answered, appearing suddenly behind them. "I felt somehow that I was superfluous—not entirely welcome—and when you left it became more pronounced than ever. But now that you are back I'm ordering a treat for us all. Be here in just a moment, and I defy Miss Stony Heart there to refuse my peace offering, though what I have done to require a peace offering beats me. Suppose you tell me, Marshall. Miss Barker seems unwilling to talk to me, except when she is on duty and is required to do so. Tell me how I have offended, if I have, or is it that I am anathema to the lady?"

"Don't be an idiot, Dr. Channing," came surprisingly from Barker. "What could you have done?"

"Then why am I in the doghouse?"

"I wasn't aware that you were," she told him evenly, still unsmiling.

"Shall I leave again?" Kathy asked demurely.

"Don't you dare!" Irene hissed.

"No for heaven's sake stay and protect me, Marshall," the man pleaded. "Anything could happen to me in her present mood." He proceeded to pile Kathy's purchases on the floor beside his chair and sat down, this time a little closer to Barker than before. Kathy grinned at her friend and shook her head.

"I hate male flirts," Barker muttered, her cheeks hot.

"Surely you can't accuse me of anything so utterly low and common as flirting, Barker," the man whispered. "Honestly, I can't understand you. Tell me why you hate me. Is it something I lack, some manly attribute? Is it that I am too tall, perhaps; too lanky; too shy; or too aggressive? Is it that I am contented to remain a Resident here, under—or apparently under—the thumb of the Chief, instead of taking a practice some place and working on my own? Is that it, Irene?" If he realized that he had used her first name he didn't show it, and while Barker flushed a deeper red she made no sign except to put out her hand to him. They were oblivious of a third person, and when the two clasped hands and smiled into each other's eyes, Kathy gave a long sigh of relief.

"Well," she murmured devoutly, "it's about time. Here you were, two of the people I most admire, at swords' points over nothing. Let's be friends from now on. No more suspicions, no more misunderstandings. It's getting late. I'll run along, and you can come when you want to. Good-by. See you at breakfast, Irene." And before the older nurse could do more than make a weak protest, the girl had fled, leaving her parcels for Dr. Channing to retrieve.

She had gone but a few steps when a car drew up beside her and a gay voice hailed her. "Hi, Kathy!" Butch Adams called. "I've been looking all over creation for you. How does it happen you're out alone?"

Kathy laughed. "Irene Barker is in there having ice cream with Dr. Channing," she explained. "They didn't need me, so I left. Want to make something of it?" she challenged, as he so often did.

"Sure I do. I'm here to kidnap you. Dana misses you. Her family isn't enough and she wants you, too, so I'm here to bring you home. In fact she told me not to return without you. Pete, the big stiff, wanted to come with me but I shoved off without him. What has Pete got that I haven't, except a year or two, and what do they amount to? Time'll take care of that all right. Hop in, Kathy, and we'll be off."

"Like this, Butch?" the girl demurred. "I can't go to a party in this outfit."

"What's the matter with it?" the boy demanded. "You'd

61

look good to me in a potato sack. It isn't a party anyway. Don't be funny, Baby. No one's dolled up. It's you Dana wants, not your clothes. Warm enough? Wrap that robe around your knees—no, here let me do it. I'm used to mothering dames."

Kathy laughed again. "I bet you are," she jibed. "They learn young in the east, I've discovered. How old are you, Butch?"

"Years don't mean a thing, Kathy. In experience and actual brains I'm much older than you are, and what's more I intend showing you that I can outsmart and out-maneuver Dr. MacDonald or any old pill dispenser in this man's town. Don't you get sick of doctors, Kathy? Just now Dana's ga-ga over Mac. Well, he's not a bad guy as doctor's go, but I feel she could do better—with her legs, you know."

"Legs, Butch?" Kathy asked, startled.

"Sure, legs. Sis is a dancer, you know. I bet she would make a killing on the stage if it wasn't for Gram. Pete and I are teaching her to walk, and she is trying mighty hard. But the poor kid's scared to put her full weight on her legs, although we—and the Doc, too—assured her that her legs are as strong or stronger than they ever were. But she'll learn, she's got to," he said fiercely.

"Of course she will," Kathy told him, as they sped along in the frosty January night.

The Hammond house was alight from top to bottom. The Christmas wreaths, hung rather belatedly, were still in the windows, giving a holiday air to the big place, and once again Kathy felt a wave of nostalgia as she thought of her own faraway home and all those she held dear. But once inside her spirits lifted, and she discovered with something of relief that Dr. MacDonald was not present. Dana looked better and insisted that Kathy be shown all the gifts she had received from friends and neighbors.

"And guess what?" she cried, as the nurse exclaimed and admired the display. "My boss at the plant sent me an album of dance music, 'to inspire me,' he said." The brown eyes filled with tears, through which she smiled bravely. "I play them over and over again, but somehow my feet don't seem to want to follow."

"But of course they will, Dana," Kathy told her with sincerity. "Have you taken any steps at all? You have been home two weeks and over, haven't you? After all, it hasn't been very long. You mustn't rush things."

The girl dashed a hand across her eyes and nodded. "That's what the doctor tells me. Butch insists that I did walk alone, but I think he was just saying that to encourage me. I can't believe it."

"O.K.," her brother said, "let's prove it." He took both her hands and pulled her to her feet and walking backward and humming softly the air of a favorite waltz, he held his sister erect and with Pete close beside her, to give her confidence, he slowly walked her across the room where she sank into a chair, laughing and crying by turns.

Kathy clapped her hands while the others cried, "Bravo!"

"But—but I didn't do it alone, Butch," Dana protested. "I held on to your hands like grim death."

"You did nothing of the sort," her brother denied. "I scarcely felt your hands at all. You're a dancer, Sis. You've got rhythm. Don't forget that. Now want to try it again? You walk over to Kathy. Pete and I will see that you don't fall. But we won't touch you. O.K.? Up you go. Right, left, right—fine!" and he began to sing, keeping time to the girl's faltering steps.

Kathy caught Dana's hands, as she reached the sofa, and drew her down beside her.

"That was wonderful!" the nurse told her enthusiastically. "I have never heard of anyone who walked alone as quickly as you have. I'm very happy for you, darling!" she whispered, her arm about the excited girl.

"I did it, didn't I?" Dana gasped in her excitement. "Gram, did you see? I did it, I walked alone! I wish the doctor were here. Wouldn't he be surprised? He has kept telling me to take it easy, that I wasn't going anywhere so there was no need of haste, but he doesn't realize how badly I want to walk, run, dance as I did before. What's the matter, Butch?" she asked her younger brother, who seemed to be leaning for support against Peter.

"Nothing," the boy gulped. "Only, I—I guess I was scared. I'm a dope!"

"No more walking for Dana tonight," Mrs. Hammond said firmly.

"It's getting rather late," Kathy murmured, getting to her feet, "and I think Dana should be in bed. Did the doctor leave you sedatives, Mrs. Hammond? I think one wouldn't hurt her right now. She's excited and I doubt if she will sleep, but bed is the best place for her. It has been wonderful being here. I miss my own people, at times like these, and you were kind to invite me."

"The pleasure is all ours," Butch said glibly, while Mrs. Hammond took the girl's hand in hers.

"I hope you will come often, my dear. We are all very fond of you, you know, and we should like you to look upon us as family and upon our home as your own. Drive carefully, Butch—oh, is it Peter going with you? Well, you drive carefully too, dear," she told her elder grandson, amused at the disgruntled expression on Butch's face.

Outside in the cold winter darkness, Kathy felt again the friendly interest and warmth she had experienced ever since meeting the Adams family and their charming grandmother. Peter wrapped the robe snugly about her knees, and while he was less talkative than his brother he made the drive interesting with stories of the family, whom he frankly adored. He told her of Dana's dancing success but showed his displeasure at the idea of her making it her career.

"Just now she's infatuated with her doctor, which I suppose is quite natural. He has been pretty wonderful to her—to us all, for that matter. Gram sort of encourages it. You see, Gram and Mrs. MacDonald are close friends, and I have a notion they talk about it. Of course I don't know. Maybe they don't. After all, Dana's only twenty-two, a mere kid still, and Doc must be in his thirties. How does he stand with the staff at Memorial, Kathy?" he asked tentatively.

"Very well, I imagine," the girl said briefly.

"Oh, Dana's crush is probably nothing more than that —a crush. When she gets back on her feet and is able to date some of the old crowd, it will probably die a natural death. . . . Do you like MacDonald, Kathy?"

Kathy could feel the quick blood rush to her cheeks, but she managed to answer with what she hoped was cool indifference.

"Of course I like him. We all like him. He is kind, thoughtful, and cooperative, and to nurses that means a lot from a doctor. Some of them are quite the reverse, I assure you."

"Do you enjoy nursing, Kathy?" the young man persisted. "Lots of doctors marry nurses, don't they? There was a time when Dana was quite jealous of you, you know. But I guess she heard it was some other doctor you were interested in. Tell me it is none of my business, Kathy," he said quickly, and as she didn't reply he went on hesitantly but with an air of do-or-die grimness. "You see, I have fallen pretty hard for you and—and the idea of all those doctors sort of—well, gives me the jitters. I've got a couple more years in college, darling, and I'm sure I can take care of you. Will you give me a chance, Kathy? You're so lovely, so dear, I—we all love you."

Kathy laid a hand on the arm nearest her and said softly, "Thank you, Peter. You're sweet! I'm much too old for you, you know, but it is wonderful to feel that you like me—that your family likes me. But I have no thought of marrying anyone—at least not for a long time. You are very young, dear, but I want you to know that you have paid me the highest compliment any woman can receive."

"So your answer is 'no'?" the boy said unhappily.

"It must be 'no', Peter," Kathy told him softly. "I'm sorry, for I love you and all your family. You have helped me through the holidays when I have missed my own people."

"Tell me," the young man said, after a moment. "Is there anyone else? Are you promised to any other man?"

Kathy shook her head. "No, Peter," she told him promptly. "Marriage is the farthest thing from my mind. I love my work, and I hope to devote my life to nursing."

There was a deep sigh from the young man beside her, and Kathy looked at him in surprise.

"Well," Peter said grimly, "I shall not give up. I—I don't suppose you will let me kiss you?"

And Kathy, who was beginning to feel slightly hysterical, shook her head and slipped from the car, although she knew that the young man, being well brought up, would feel cheated of his manly privilege and obligation to help her out and escort her to the annex. But she had no desire to hurt him and felt sure there was danger of it if she lingered, as the entire proceedings had begun to appear ridiculous.

And yet even after she was in bed she didn't laugh.

Somehow Peter was so much in earnest—so sincere—that while the entire affair appeared fantastic she felt a great sympathy for the boy, experiencing his first love affair, possibly heartbreak. She found it anything but funny. Poor Peter! she murmured, as she dozed off. Poor darling Peter! And poor Kathy too, who, while feeling confident that she was completely untouched by Gary MacDonald's evident love for Dana Adams, yet experienced a sense of loss. He had been attracted to *her* before the advent of Dana. Poor Kathy, she whispered, and slept.

CHAPTER EIGHT

How is 312 GETTING on, Kathy?" Irene Barker asked, as the two nurses met in the practically empty bathroom early one morning. "Someone mentioned the fact that she is a maniac depressive. If that is true, she should not be here. Why on earth did they assign you to the case, Kathy? And do you mind?"

Kathy Marshall shook her head, although she looked troubled. "Miss Parker? I have heard stories about her," she said. "She is depressed, and I'm of the opinion that it is the result of some personal tragedy, mental or physical. I can find out little about her background. No one seems to know. The poor thing is quite alone in the world, and yet she is not old—not more than forty—and must have been pretty, or at least nice-looking, once upon a time. I haven't been able to find out anything from her. She mutters to herself but will scarcely answer when anyone talks to her. It's an interesting case, Irene," the girl went on. "I'm going to find out how I can help her. I'm not sorry for the three months I spent in a psychiatric hospital. We had worse psychotics there, and many of them recovered."

"I don't care for mentally ill patients," the older nurse murmured.

"That's because you never worked among them as I did," Kathy replied. "Some of them were especially pathetic types; some of them realized, in a measure, their condition and strove desperately to orient themselves. That is where a nurse comes in. It's our job to help, to bring them out of the fog that shadows their minds into the clear light of day. I found it fascinating. It's hard work, sometimes appearing almost hopeless, but after I had seen several regain their reason and walk out normal human beings, I began to take heart—to have more patience and hope. No, I don't consider 312 a maniac type at all."

"Is she a native of Bostwick, Kathy?"

"I don't think so. I have an idea she came here to lose herself, to get away from something or someone responsible for her melancholy. I may be wrong, of course, but that's how I feel, and Dr. Channing thinks I may be right."

"But who brought her here? How did she happen to land in Memorial in the first place?

"Dr. MacDonald said the landlady sent for him when Miss Parker fell from a chair and hit her head against a dresser in her apartment. I was a little surprised, because I thought Dr. MacDonald specialized in surgery, didn't you?"

Irene Barker shook her head. "Not exclusively, Kathy. I understand he is both a physician and surgeon, although he made a special study of the latter. It seems he dislikes the term 'specialist'; he prefers to be known as a plain, honest-to-goodness doctor. More power to him, I say. Somehow we've become specialized to death these days. And what does MacDonald have to say about 312?"

"Not a great deal," Kathy answered. "He told me the patient should be closely watched and to see that she remained as quiet as possible. I have an idea he thinks as the Resident and I do. It seems she has acted moody ever since she came here—to town, I mean. Mrs. Meredith, her landlady, thought she behaved strangely—'decidedly odd' was the way she put it. Miss Parker hád no callers and no mail—seemed to shun people. She refused to visit with the talkative landlady, and I suppose that was annoying. If asked a question, she answered civilly enough, but tersely, so that people came to avoid her. It was apparent that she was a woman of means; she lived well, and her clothes—trust the neighbors to know that—were beautiful. But she seldom left her apartment. She bought a small car when she first came to Bostwick but drove it very little. It's a strange case, Irene," Kathy murmured, "and I should like to know just what is troubling her. It seems the doctor she called in one evening, when she was not feeling well, told Mrs. Meredith that she was a neurotic old maid. And that is all that Dr. MacDonald had to go on."

67

"She has one of the best rooms here," Irene reminded the other, musingly. "Someone is responsible. Old tight-as-a-drum Blaine would never stand for that unless he knew the money was forthcoming to pay her bill."

"I don't know. She appears well cared for—her body, I mean. Her hands are slim and white, and her hair clean, and she must recently have had a permanent, although her hair might be naturally curly. It's pretty, anyway—a deep reddish brown. I can't overcome the feeling that there is a reason for her melancholy, and I am going to try to find out what it is and help remedy it."

"Little Miss Fix-it," chided her friend.

"I don't care," Kathy retorted. "She needs help, and I'm going to give her what I can."

"You say she isn't married?"

"That's the story. She doesn't wear a wedding ring, but that doesn't necessarily mean anything. Lots of people don't wear them for some reason. She was entered as unmarried and that, too, doesn't mean too much, does it?"

The older nurse shook her head. "Do you know, you have awakened my interest in 312, Kathy," she said after a minute. "If you find out anything, let me know; and if there is anything I can do to help, I'm your girl."

The two finished their ablutions and returned to their rooms, then met again just outside Kathy's door to go down to breakfast together. Nothing more was said about the patient in 312, and after the morning meal Kathy, who was now on day duty, left her friend when the elevator stopped at the third floor and walked along to her patient's room. Morton, the night nurse, made a brief entry on the chart and turned as the day nurse entered the room. The patient lay as she so often did, with her face to the wall, and if she was awake or asleep, Kathy didn't know.

"No change," Liz Morton muttered, as she handed the chart to her relief and prepared to leave the room. "It sure has been plenty dreary around here. Just what do you suppose ails the woman, Marshall?"

"She's sick," Kathy replied softly, and examined the chart while the night nurse went out, letting the door close softly behind her. She busied herself about the room for a few minutes, then walked over to the narrow bed. "Good morning, Miss Parker," she said. "Feeling better?"

68

"I shall never feel better," the patient murmured drearily. "Leave me alone. I'm sick of life."

"Well, then," the nurse advised, "let's see what we can do about it. A nice warm bath followed by an alcohol rub will help, I'm sure, and then breakfast. Is there anything you would like this morning? Tell me and I will try to get it for you."

Hilda Parker turned slowly and stared at the girl beside the bed. "Why do you bother?" she asked tonelessly.

"It's no bother," Kathy told her gently. "It's my job, you know, and I love it."

There was a short bitter sound from the patient that, Kathy thought, was meant for laughter. "Love taking care of sick and disagreeable people? You don't expect me to believe that."

"And why not?" Kathy asked, smiling. "I trained for it—put in three long years in learning to become a nurse. I didn't have to, you know. There are many other professions I could have entered, but I chose nursing. You look better this morning. I hope you slept well."

"Sleep?" the woman muttered. "I never sleep. Oh, I wish I were dead. Life is over for me; it is meaningless, worthless. I don't want to live—to exist—to suffer."

"Do you want to tell me about it?" Kathy asked tentatively. "Sometimes talking to someone helps, you know, and I do want to help you. Just a moment while I get your bath water and towels." She left the room, returned with the necessary paraphernalia for a bath, and went on, "Have you been ill, Miss Parker, or recently lost someone dear to you? After your bath I shall change your sheets and put a fresh gown on you. It is amazing how such trivial things can alter one's outlook on life. You know, my dear, everyone has to face loss, disappointment, and discouragement at times."

"Did you?" the woman asked skeptically.

"Yes," Kathy answered softly. "Although I suppose people would laugh at my troubles, they were very real to me."

The woman looked disdainful. "But you're young, you are lovely, you haven't really lived," she muttered. "Did you ever have to suffer betrayal—ridicule and desertion —by the only one who made life worth-while? Did you ever watch the disintegration, the complete wreckage, of the character of a fine man? Watch him become the puppet of a vile unprincipled woman? No, I'll guarantee that you haven't, and God grant you never will."

"Your husband?"

"The man I married," the woman muttered bitterly. "He was never really my husband. He married me for my inheritance—for my beautiful home, my social position. I was weak enough to love him and he, for a time, played the part of a devoted husband."

"Have you children, Miss—Mrs. Parker?" Kathy asked.

The woman shook her head. Her face was suddenly sad. "No, Tim never seemed to want children, and I—I——"

She began to weep quickly and devastatingly, and Kathy put her arms about her and held her gently as a mother might until the paroxysm passed.

"Now," she said, handing her a square of tissue, "blow your nose and you'll feel better. You are a very lucky woman, Mrs. Parker——"

"Don't call me that," the patient said fiercely. "I'm Miss Parker. Tim's name was Arnold, a hateful name and one I shall never use again." She gulped once or twice and then managed a wry grin. "Do you have to listen to many confessions, Nurse?" she asked almost apologetically.

"Of course," Kathy replied quietly. "You know nurses are like doctors, ministers, and priests. We listen, do what we can to help, and lock the confidences in our hearts. Have you been divorced?"

The woman shook her head vigorously. "No. Tim is a menace. He should not be allowed to ruin any other woman's life."

"Then you still love him?" the nurse asked, almost fearfully.

Miss Parker stared at her for a long moment before she asked scornfully, "Is that what you think? Did you draw that conclusion from what I told you? No. I hate him! I loathe him! I never want to see him again—and," she added forlornly, "I probably never shall."

"Now for breakfast," the nurse said, deftly patting the patient's face with a powder puff. "Grapefruit, coffee, toast, bacon, perhaps, and scrambled eggs? You have been dieting unnecessarily since you have been here. Goodness knows you're slim enough. Anything else?"

70

"Heavens!" the woman cried, and this time the mouth was really smiling. "What do you think I am? I never eat breakfast. Oh, a glass of orange juice, perhaps, and a cup of black coffee, but nothing else. I have always been a little proud of my figure, Nurse, and lying in bed like this I don't require much. Do you know," she said musingly, "I like it here. You're sweet, and I think I shall stay for a few days. How did I come to be here anyway? Oh, I remember. I fell, didn't I, and I suppose I scared Mrs. Meredith. But my head still hurts. Did that fall make a bump? Yes, it did, I can feel it."

"It's a beautiful bump, Miss Parker," the nurse told her, "and a fascinating shade of purple just now. I imagine it knocked you out for a while, but no real damage was done. Were you dizzy, or what happened?"

"I hadn't eaten anything for hours, and I was straightening a shade and then suddenly everything swam before my eyes and the floor came up to meet me. I am not a fainting woman, Nurse," she said whimsically, "and have always prided myself on having poise and complete control of my reflexes—although," she went on, a note of annoyance in her voice, "I heard one of the doctors say I was a maniac depressive or something like that. What did he mean, Nurse? I wasn't supposed to hear, but he shouldn't have talked so loud—or talked at all for that matter. I'm not at all neurotic, Nurse, if that is what he meant. Or was it something worse?"

"He was probably not talking about you at all," Kathy temporized. She had never approved of discussing patients' conditions in corridors or anywhere that there was the least possibility of a patient's overhearing.

"Oh, yes he was," the woman persisted, "but I didn't care. I felt far too miserable, and my head was splitting. Maniac depressive indeed! What's that, anyway? Sounds crazy, and I assure you that I am very far from insane."

"I'm sure you are," Kathy told her soothingly. "Now you relax and rest while I see about your breakfast. The trays should be along very soon now, but I think I shall go down to the kitchen for yours this morning."

"You're nice," the woman murmured, and turned on her side, her face to the wall.

Kathy raised the shades to let in the early gray of the winter morning before she left the room. She wished she

71

knew who the doctor was who had talked so loudly about her patient.

She met Dr. Channing as he left the elevator, and he stopped for a moment to ask about the condition of 312.

"Much improved this morning," Kathy told him, wondering whether to report the infringement of rules regarding idle discussions of patients within their hearing.

"Dr. Alcott, her physician—at least he calls himself her physician, having been called to treat her one evening for some minor ailment—reported the possibility of a psychosis, Marshall, possibly manic depression. What do you think? I know you worked with that type while you were in training. Has she shown evidence of anything of the sort? We can't handle cases of that kind here, you know."

"She's all right, Doctor," Kathy assured him. "She's an unhappy woman, that's all that's the matter with her. She unloaded it all on me this morning, and as we have been told that confession is good for the soul I assure you it is definitely good for the mind and body as well. But I'm glad to know it was no member of our staff who talked outside her door yesterday while she was supposed to be unconscious."

"Why? Who said what? Was she upset? We try to avoid such things, Marshall, although they do happen sometimes. What was it that she heard?"

"That she was a manic depressive, and she thought it meant she was crazy. She likes it here and has decided to remain for a few days until the lump on her head is reduced. I like her, Dr. Channing," Kathy went on. "Life has treated her badly."

"We have discovered that she has plenty of money— at least the Chief made it his business to find out her financial status."

"Bostwick Memorial should have a business manager," Kathy laughed, "and then he wouldn't have to concern himself about finances."

"Oh yes he would," the Resident said emphatically. "He couldn't help himself. I'll stop in at 312 and see how she treats me. I have an idea she's not partial to doctors, Marshall."

"I'm on my way to take her breakfast to her myself this morning, Doctor," the nurse said. "She doesn't want much, just orange juice and clear coffee. Yes, she's a member of the 'no breakfast' sorority, although I can't see the necessity in her particular case. But"—she shrugged—"it takes all sorts, doesn't it?"

Dr. Channing nodded. "I'm glad you called it a sorority instead of a fraternity, Marshall," he smiled. "Men have too much sense to miss their breakfast. Most of them make it their best meal of the day and quite rightly, too, from a health standpoint."

"Oh, men!" Kathy scoffed, as she left him.

Down in the diet kitchen the specials were busy preparing trays for their patients while the general duty nurses assisted the maids in loading the carts with the regulation breakfasts. It didn't take Kathy long to place a glass of orange juice and a pot of coffee on a tray and start to leave.

"Hi!" one of the specials called to her. "Who've you got? Look at my load. He'll eat us out of house and home if he stays here much longer. Look at it, will you?" she urged, pointing to the laden tray. "Grapefruit, well sweetened; a pot of coffee, a big pot at that; fresh rolls, three of 'em; two three-minute eggs; a dozen rashers of bacon; two fried cakes; and—oh yes, cream and sugar just in case. Gosh, Marshall, I hope I don't meet the Chief or he'll confiscate the entire meal."

"Who is he?" Kathy laughed. "At least there's nothing wrong with his appetite."

"Never has been," his special replied. "He's Mike Burlison, boss of the Northern Lights Lumber Company over on the north side. Weighs nearly three hundred and stands six feet three in his socks. At least that's what he told me; I've never seen him perpendicular yet. He's a good patient, though, only he has too much company—for his nurse, I mean. Company doesn't seem to hurt him any, although the Chief tried to curtail it. You should have heard Mike put him in his place. It did my heart good. He's here for a broken kneecap. Painful but not too serious. Going up, Marshall? I'll go along as far as the second floor."

The elevator was at the seventh floor, evidently being held for some reason, and Manning, the special, groaned and rested her laden tray on a nearby stand. Kathy was deciding to walk the three flights to her patient, when the elevator began to whirr and started down with only two or three stops, and the girls prepared to enter as it halted before them. Dr. MacDonald and the Chief of Staff stepped out.

The older man caught sight of the heavily laden tray and growled, "Have we a gourmand among our patients? Is all that food for one person, Manning?"

"Well, Doctor," the girl answered hesitantly, "at least he has a good appetite."

"Good! So much food—why, it's outrageous, unheard of. Who is this patient, Nurse? It must stop at once. Who did you say?"

"211, Doctor, Mi-Mr. Burlison. It's what he ordered."

Kathy's quizzical gaze met the twinkling eyes of Gary MacDonald, and she bit her lip to prevent laughing.

"Oh," the Chief muttered, as he strode off down the corridor, followed by the frankly smiling junior surgeon. Martha Manning wrinkled her pert nose after them, and Kathy pressed the button, as the two nurses entered the now empty elevator.

CHAPTER NINE

SEVERAL DAYS PASSED BEFORE Mrs. Arnold—or Miss Parker as she pereferred to be known—again mentioned her personal woes to her nurse, and Kathy watched her slow improvement under the care and attention she received at the hospital. Irene Barker asked from time to time what more was known about her, and then one day the patient in 312 became talkative. Her tone was far less bitter than heretofore, and the nurse knew an upsurge of relief.

"Do you know, Kathy," the patient said one morning, as the nurse settled her in a comfortable chair before a window where she could look out on the snowy landscape. "I have become a bit curious about Tim—if he's at all puzzled at my disappearance. I wonder if he is worried," she went on, and Kathy detected a trace of doubt in the woman's voice, as if she almost wished that he had worried and had begun searching for her. "But I suppose that is asking too much of such a dignified yet self-centered man as Tim Arnold, and anyway, I don't imagine his paramour would stand for it. I'm a fool, Kathy," she went on quickly, almost apologetically. "Other woman have fought to keep their men, and have succeeded, but I suppose I was too proud or too stubborn to make the attempt. If there had been children, no doubt I should have tried to hold our home together, but—oh, I don't know! Doubt is like a ravaging disease. It eats into one's soul and destroys one. Once opening the door of one's heart to suspicion and doubt is simply inviting misery and woe to become permanent occupants. All my life I've been a fool, such a blind fool. Oh, Kathy, I've made such a mess of my life!"

Hilda Parker and her nurse had grown fond of each other, and the older woman followed Kathy's instructions implicitly, even to eating a reasonable breakfast each morning. Both nurse and patient found the result gratifying, though of course there had been arguments.

"But suppose I gain weight," the patient had asked dubiously.

"You could stand ten pounds, Miss Parker," Kathy had told her. "You are taller than I am, and yet you weigh fifteen pounds less. I'm not a pound overweight, and I eat my breakfast and enjoy it. You see, I grew up on a farm in Wisconsin, and in the country we like good substantial breakfasts. Try it and see what happens. I don't think you will get fat, only you will feel better—peppier."

"Well," the woman had agreed. "Only you're young, and I'm getting on in years."

Kathy had laughed merrily. "You're lovely, at the most charming and attractive period of your life. Make the most of it, my dear."

And now, this wintry morning with snow blowing in gusts against the windows, Hilda Parker stretched her slim arms above her head and yawned as she hadn't done since her arrival at Bostwick Memorial. She had been walking about her room, and even strolling into the sun room at the end of the long corridor. In her mink coat, over satin pajamas and velvet housecoat—she had from the first refused to use hospital garb—she had become an interesting and familiar figure to the staff and the patients.

"Honestly, Irene," Kathy told her friend, as they sat in the latter's room before going on duty, "I don't understand why she stays on here. I can't see but what she is perfectly well. She even talks now about her errant husband; talks almost indulgently, at least far less bitterly.

75

"Just where does she come from, Kathy?" Irene wanted to know, buffing her nails vigorously. "Did she tell you?"

"Oh, yes. She owns a home in Rumsey, Connecticut. I don't imagine Rumsey is a very large town, and from what she told me her people, the Parkers, are among the first families. Why?"

"Rumsey, Connecticut?" Irene exclaimed. "Why, that's where Joan Wells lives. She was before your time, but she was and is a grand girl. She married George Howard, who interned here back in the dark ages. I got a card from her at Christmas, inviting me to come up for my vacation. What a coincidence! How would it be if I wrote Joanie and made some confidential inquiries regarding this—this Tim Arnold? Would it help, do you think?"

"It might," Kathy said, then added dubiously, "that is, if he isn't tied up with a hussy, like his wife thinks he is. It wouldn't do any harm to try," she went on with sudden enthusiasm. "Wouldn't it be wonderful if things could be ironed out between them? I like Hilda Parker, Irene, and I feel terribly sorry for her. Let's get busy.

Irene Barker laughed. "You're still Little Miss Fix-it, Kathy," she chided affectionately. "And I'm going to tell you something. This too is confidential. Bob Channing is showing definite signs of courting me. Oh, I assure you it is all very circumspect and in keeping with our positions here in Memorial, but just the same the signs are there and believe me they aren't hard to take. I'll skip across to my room and get that note off to Joanie. I'll hear almost at once. She's that sort. See you later, Kathy," she added, as the door closed behind her, and Kathy smiled to herself and wondered just what the result would be.

It was two days later that she found out. While the patient in 312 and her nurse were deep in the intricacies of a new jigsaw puzzle that Miss Parker had charmed the Resident into bringing to her, a faint knock on the closed door sent Kathy to answer it. A tall, gray-haired man of middle age stood in the corridor and then, with a muttered word of apology, brushed her aside and strode into the room. Kathy turned indignantly, but before she could do more than open her mouth there came a gasp of astonishment from her patient and a cry of relief from the visitor as he swept aside table and puzzle and caught the white-faced woman in a close embrace.

"What do you mean by frightening me out of my wits, Hilda Arnold?" he demanded fiercely. "Why did you do it? Why, why, why?" All the time, he was pressing her head against his shoulder, and Kathy wondered if those were tears of anger or joy that filled his eyes.

Hilda Parker tried to draw away, but the man held her tightly and said raggedly, "No, you don't ever gain. But tell me why you ran away. What did I do?"

"That woman!" his wife muttered.

"What woman?" the man demanded. "There has never been any woman but you. Is it that you don't love me, can't stand having me around any longer, darling? Don't you care that I worship you, that I have tried in every way I know to win your love in return?"

The head pressed so tightly against his shoulder drew back, and the startled eyes stared into his for a long moment while Kathy stood transfixed against the door. Should she remain just in case of fireworks, or should she leave them to a grand reunion?

Before she could move, her patient whispered, "Love, Tim? Do you mean to say that you actually love me? That——"

"Of course I love you, silly," he told her. "Why have you been so cold, so suspicious, so stand-offish all these years? Is it your money, Hilda? Your boasted ancestry? Your social position in Rumsey? It has hurt and puzzled me. I'm just a simple chap, darling?"

"Tim," a low voice said, and as Kathy opened the door and slipped into the corridor, the voice went on, "I'm ashamed. . . ."

Perhaps an hour later Kathy was summoned to 312, where she met the smiling Mrs. Arnold and her equally happy husband.

"Was it you who did it, Kathy?" her patient said. "Somehow I had an idea you were something of a good fairy, my dear."

"I'm so happy for you both," the nurse said. "But it was not I who brought your husband to Bostwick, Mrs. Arnold," she explained. "That was simply Fate."

"We want to get out of here as soon as possible, Nurse," the beaming husband said, his arm about his wife. "Is Hilda—Mrs. Arnold—able to leave the hospital?"

"I'm perfectly well, Tim," his wife said.

Kathy agreed with her. "I think it can be taken care of," she told them, and she departed to make the necessary arrangements.

And so it was that Kathy lost one of her favorite patients. Having watched them leave with a feeling of happy accomplishment, she waited until Irene Barker came to her room sometime later and then told her of the happy ending of the story.

"It was hard for me to believe Mr. Arnold was the philandering male his wife insisted he was," Kathy said, as she finished recounting the episode. "He appeared deeply in love with his wife, and I wonder if it wasn't largely due to her unresponsiveness that he seemed indifferent and even wandering in his search for the understanding companionship she must have denied him. Well, I certainly hope they have no more upheavals, Irene. Anyway, Mrs. Arnold is in much better health than when she arrived here several weeks ago. That's what a good breakfast does for you." She laughed, pointing an accusing finger at her friend, who lately had been skipping breakfast in the hope of losing weight.

Irene shook her head. "It's all right for you to talk, Kathy Marshall," she chided. "You're young. Probably you don't put on weight with every ounce of sweets or spoonful of cream you eat. But I do. Let me take sugar and cream in my morning coffee and wham! up goes my weight. And where does it all land? Right on my hips. Well, I've lost six pounds since I swore off breakfasts.

In her turn Kathy shook her head. "Just the same," she insisted, "I feel sure you could reduce in some other way—go light on other meals, perhaps, avoid desserts at dinner, cut out the candy you're so fond of. In fact you might even halve your other meals, but darling, you need your breakfast. A good one, too, if you want to keep well. What does Dr. Channing say about your dieting? I bet he wouldn't approve if he knew it."

"And don't you dare tell him, Kathy Marshall," Irene cried. "I hope some bright day to have his gaze follow me as approvingly as it does some of the slim-jims we have here in the hospital. Even you, my child, get that approving eye from our Resident. I'm going to win it or die in the attempt," she added fiercely.

Kathy laughed. "And if you acquire wrinkles, what will you do?"

"I won't," the other promised. "Anyway, it's one's figure that counts, that gets the admiring whistle and the acquisitive eye, darling, and I intend winning both. Anyway, all the beauticians tell us if we want to reduce it must be before forty. Well, I've a few years to go before I reach that deadline, and believe me I intend playing safe. So, go on preaching and practicing the good breakfast policy. I'll stick to my fast." She examined her plump self in the mirror and sighed dolefully. "Darn it!" she groaned after a minute, "why does it take so long?"

"Don't worry," Kathy told her comfortingly. "Six pounds in ten days is extraordinary. I doubt if you can keep it up. Two or three pounds a week is considered a safe reduction."

"To change the subject," Irene said, her critical eye still on the mirror. "How is the Adams girl coming along with her walking?"

"Good, from what I have heard," Kathy told her. "She can get around the house all right with only slight help, but she still fears the stairs and walking alone for any distance. She doesn't limp, at least not much, and wants to go back to work. Her grandmother thinks she should stay at home for the remainder of the winter, but Dana insists that she should be able to go back after the first of the month. I don't know, though. There are stairs to climb—short flights, to be sure, but still stairs. The company has offered to send a car for her in the morning and bring her back at night, but Mrs. Hammond still demurs, though I don't think they have too much money, and Dana feels she should be helping."

"Have you heard any more about her and Gary MacDonald, Kathy?" Irene asked.

Kathy shook her head. "Her brother Peter hinted about an attachment there, but I wouldn't know. Dana hasn't said anything to me about it, and Dr. MacDonald seems to be quite preoccupied with his job. Anyway she's very young, she appears much younger than her years, while Dr. MacDonald seems much older. Have you heard how he and the Chief are getting along these days? I haven't seen much of either one lately."

"I have a notion MacDonald is keeping out of the

79

Chief's way as much as possible," the older nurse said, "although I came upon them in consultation over the Alnutt case just yesterday. You know, Jay Alnutt is the dairy farmer who was gored by his pure-blooded, registered bull last month and nearly lost his life because he refused to allow the hired man who came to his rescue to shoot the animal. Lucky for him the family bulldog, an old fellow, appeared on the scene and grabbed the lower lip of the infuriated beast as he lowered his head for the final attack. The dog hung on like grim death, almost tearing away the entire lower jaw. While that was going on, and the maddened bull was trying desperately to shake himself loose, the farm hands managed to drag Alnutt to safety. They tell me that even then it was next to impossible to separate the dog and the bull. Believe it or not, Kathy, it was the six-year-old daughter who managed the trick. She went out to the fence and screamed at the dog —Duke, I believe his name is—until he let go, and when the big animal swung his head, Duke dropped outside the fence. The powers that be wished that case on me this morning. I didn't want it, but the Chief insisted."

Irene paused.

"I'm fed up on doing special work, Kathy," she went on. "I want a turn at either general duty or ward work. Even a few days of Pediatrics wouldn't come amiss just now. I guess I need a vacation. This place is getting on my nerves!"

"How badly is Mr. Alnutt injured, Irene?" Kathy asked.

"A couple of broken ribs, a lacerated hip, multiple bruises, and a badly dislocated disposition. And believe it or not, his concern is almost wholly for that cantankerous bull. Can you bear it? He declares Bertrand—that's the animal's name, or one of 'em; he has a string of ten or a dozen on his pedigree—has always been gentle as a kitten."

"There's no such thing as a gentle or harmless bull, Irene," the younger nurse asserted positively. "I know. I was brought up on a farm, and I have heard plenty about bulls and their idiosyncrasies. A gentle bull? 'There ain't no such animal.' That's a slogan in my part of the country, and I've heard farmers warned time and again by men who know. If Mr. Alnutt holds any such delusion he is either a moron or—or a plain fool. Is he a young man, Irene?"

"Oh, somewhere around thirty, I should say," her friend told her.

"Old enough to know better," Kathy stated positively.

"I shall take pleasure in giving him your views, Kathy." Irene laughed. "I doubt, though, if he will think much of them. He favors the younger school of thought, darling. You know, 'What I don't know about managing my own affairs isn't worth considering.' Let's not eat here tonight, Kathy. Let's go out and have a thick steak with mushrooms and all the accessories. I'm simply ravenous tonight; I could even take a bite out of the redoubtable Bertrand."

"All right," Kathy agreed. "We're having stew here anyway, and I'm not at all partial to stew à la Bostwick Memorial. Where shall we go? Dress up or ordinary?"

"Let's shoot the works, Kathy," Irene advised, her eyes shining with excitement.

"But your diet?" cautioned Kathy demurely, halting halfway in her clothes closet.

"Diet be hanged!" Irene muttered. "I'm hungry! Come on. It won't take me a minute to change. Meet me at the top of the stairs and we'll sneak out the back way. No need hurting anyone's feelings. Stew! Ugh!"

It was a cold clear night, and the two nurses hurried around the huge building to the street, where they waited for the approaching bus and rode down the long hill to the center of the city.

"We'll make a night of it, Kathy," Irene proposed. "See a movie, and even stop for hot chocolate afterward. One needs plenty of food during these cold days. Anyway, I'm six pounds to the good."

Kathy laughed merrily. "You're funny, Irene," she said, catching her friend's hand as they slid along the icy pavement to the entrance of the swank Cosmopolitan Restaurant where, in spite of the lack of reservations, the head waiter found them a table not too far from the stage.

Violinists played softly while the élite of Bostwick, apparently unmindful of the ravishing music, talked and laughed throughout the meal. The two nurses watched the diners. Irene, who knew most of the Bostwick celebrities and near celebrities, pointed them out to the younger

81

nurse, adding here and there a bit of gossip or amusing history. Kathy found it all both interesting and entertaining. Irene was a charming and witty companion, and the evening passed quickly. The dinner was good, and the two left the restaurant replete and ready for further amusement.

Just outside the door, they ran into Dr. Elliott and Dr. Channing, bound for inside and dinner.

"Why didn't you wait for us?" Dr. Elliott demanded. "We have been telephoning you since five o'clock. Where were you?"

"Oh, here and there," Irene said airily. "Run along, boys. We've dined sumptuously and are on our way to the Bijou to let Charles Boyer make us forget our troubles and charm us into the belief that there are still honest-to-goodness he-men in this cockeyed world. By now. See you sometime."

She caught Kathy's hand and pulled her along while the two young men, somewhat nonplused, watched them for a moment. Then, without a word, they went inside.

CHAPTER TEN

KATHY MARSHALL left the dining room after breakfast one day late in February with a feeling of well-being, almost exuberance. Spring seemed to have arrived overnight. When she had looked out of her bedroom window that morning, not a vestige of snow was to be seen. The air was balmy with the promise of warm sunny days ahead, and she had spotted a few hardy crocuses on the front lawn. What if pessimists loudly proclaimed the fallacy of believing in the sudden coming of spring, insisted on the danger in the welcome warmth, and even called the lovely sparkling day and golden sunshine trouble breeders? To most people, young and old alike, who had grown tired of the dreary, cold, winter months, this foretaste of warm weather was like a shot in the arm, and most of the patients in Memorial experienced lifted hearts and soaring spirits.

Kathy felt a happy little song welling up in her heart as she stopped for a moment, on her way to a new case, to wave a gay good morning to old Joseph Hadden, busily shoving the dry mop along the floor. She pushed the elevator button and waited for it to descend and then turned to hear, "So you're in luck as usual, Marshall." It was one of the older nurses, speaking almost tauntingly. "I wish you would pass on your special method of getting all the plums in this hospital. How do you do it? Apple polishing? What have you got that the rest of us lack—me, for instance? I can't understand it. Come clean, Marshall," she added crisply.

"I don't know what you're talking about, Bradley," Kathy answered. She was used to remarks like this, from a few of the nurses, and tried to ignore them.

"Oh, yes you do," the other contradicted. "Don't try playing innocent with me. We all know you have a drag. What I want to know is, where do you get it? Is it because you're pretty? Some of the other nurses are just as pretty, or even better looking. I'm serious, Marshall," she went on. "I shall keep you here until you tell me."

Kathy Marshall's gray eyes darkened, and her face flushed with annoyance. She was due on a special case, and yet she was determined to settle this question of favoritism once and for all. "You are behaving foolishly, Bradley," she said coldly. "If I appear to have a 'drag,' as you call it, it comes from the fact that I work hard and mind my own business. I try to be a good nurse, Bradley, and I feel sure that I am. Does that answer your question?"

"So," the other nurse muttered angrily, "that's to be your attitude, is it? Well, Miss High-and-mighty, you haven't heard the last of this! I happen to know a few things about you. You're not the model of decorum Merriman and the Chief think you are. What about your dates with some of the doctors? None of the rest of us can get away with it, and I'm telling you you're not going to much longer either, for I shall make it my business to see that justice is done. That's a promise, Kathy Marshall, and don't you forget it." The irate nurse rushed off before Kathy could do more than gasp her astonishment.

She was annoyed with herself for being upset. While as in all large groups of girls there were invariably a few jealous and unfriendly souls, Kathy had tried earnestly to avoid anything like friction. She had been friendly with the staff in general but, with the possible exception of Irene Barker, had made few close friends during her stay in Bostwick Memorial. Of course she was dubbed stuck-up by a few, but never before had she been classed as an apple polisher. The epithet rankled. She knew it to be unjust. At last, with a shrug designed to rid herself of the uncomfortable memory of the encounter, she stepped into the elevator and pressed the button for the fourth floor.

411A was at the end of the corridor, and the man who lay in the narrow hospital bed was thin to the point of emaciation. He was hollow-eyed, with skin like parchment Kathy felt her heart contract with pity as she stood beside him. He tried to smile at her, but the effort seemed almost more than he could endure. She had heard something of the patient's history. Addison's disease. A severe case, but fortunately not considered critical at this point. He was not a local man but his personal physician, an old doctor, had suggested his coming to Bostwick Memorial because of recent scientific discoveries being used there with marked success.

I wonder just why this case was considered such a plum, Kathy mused, as she prepared his chart and busied herself with various duties. The patient had arrived during the night, and the floor nurse had made only one entry on his chart: T, subnormal; P, hyperdicrotic; R, slow. There had been little change since the patient's arrival. Kathy knew it was going to be uphill work to prolong the life of this man, and suddenly nothing else mattered. She felt an upsurge of strength and courage for the job ahead.

Dr. Channing came into the room, as she finished the patient's morning bath, and greeted the man cordially, assuring him that he would soon be feeling better and stronger. Science had made great advances in his particular disease, and the hospital, nurses, and doctors requested his patience and complete cooperation. With difficulty the patient raised his hand, as if assuring the Resident of both, and Kathy smiled at him.

As the days lengthened into weeks, she came to admire David Amory's fortitude and courage in the face of continued weakness and heart-breaking delays. The process of dehydration seemed persistent. The adrenal cortex extract had to be administered intravenously, followed by smaller doses subcutaneously at intervals of a few hours. And through it all, the patient retained his smile of gratitude for everything his nurse and doctor tried to do.

84

Slowly, gradually, the emaciated body and weakened spirit reacted to the treatment. The patient's nausea disappeared; his appetite improved; he slept better, felt stronger, showed interest in his surroundings; his color improved.

One day he asked for a newspaper. It was his first request, and Kathy hastened to comply with it. From then on, it would be merely a matter of time and medication until David Amory was comparatively a well man again.

His convalescence was necessarily slow, and Kathy wondered why she was kept on as his special when there were so many sicker patients in the hospital and nurses were scarce. But the Resident told her that Mr. Amory insisted on retaining her and had even asked if it were possible for her to consider twelve-hour duty, for her to remain during his waking hours. Kathy's gray eyes opened wide when the Resident mentioned the patient's request. Only once before had it been made and then it had been turned down cold, but now Dr. Channing hesitated, watching her reaction.

"But, Dr. Channing," she replied, "is Mr. Amory really sick enough for that? I thought he was nearly out of the woods. And why me? I'm no better than any of the others. Oh, we get along nicely, I like him all right, but——"

"You know who he is, don't you?" the Resident asked, smiling a bit.

Kathy shook her head. "Only that his name is David Amory and that he has been a very sick man. Who is he?"

"I can't understand why you haven't heard," the Resident said, a puzzled frown on his face. "Don't tell me the nurses haven't discussed him! Even though," he added, "he has been out of the limelight for a decade at least. Hasn't Barker said anything? She must have seen him at some time."

Kathy looked mystified. "No one has talked about him to me, Doctor. Who is he? Or who was he?" she asked.

"He was once America's foremost motion picture actor. He's just past forty, Marshall, believe it or not. I'm surprised you don't remember him. How old are you, anyway?"

"Is that his stage name, Doctor?" she asked, ignoring his question. "Not that I'm familiar with all the stars by any means, but I have never heard of him, much less seen him before, although," she temporized musingly, "I can quite believe he might have been good-looking or even handsome once upon a time. Was he always so thin?"

Dr. Channing shook his head. "I'm not a movie fan myself, Marshall," he told her, "but I saw a picture of him in a magazine lately and read the accompanying article about him. According to the writer, the man was done for. Good as dead. Well, he is far from dead now and he can thank modern science, Bostwick Memorial, and you and me—in that order—that he isn't. He's really a great guy, Marshall," he went on. "I like him. But don't lose your heart to him, my girl. I've heard he's one of the world's great lovers."

"Pooh!" Kathy scoffed. "He's got to get a lot more meat on his bones before he will look the part, as far as I am concerned."

"Wait another month," the Resident told her. "He's acquiring an enormous appetite. Just now when I went in he wanted to know if he couldn't have a snack. The poor guy's hungry. I told him I would see he got it. So run down to the kitchen and bring him up a sandwich and a glass of warm milk. That should hold him until dinnertime. He asked for sherry, but I had to tell him that Bostwick Memorial is strictly teetotal—thanks to our Chief. Still, milk is better for him anyway."

Kathy left him, and downstairs in the kitchen she encountered Miss Merriman. "I should like you to come to my office during your afternoon rest period, Marshall," the Superintendent of Nurses said quietly.

"Yes, Miss Merriman," Kathy answered. She wondered if she was to be transferred to another patient. Well, she didn't mind. She didn't think much of being on twelve-hour duty, even though the patient was undemanding and the work far from arduous. Bostwick Memorial was rather strict in adhering to the eight-hour schedule for its staff, but there had been times when schedules were forgotten in the stress of nurse shortages and much sickness. She wondered idly who her next patient was to be and wondered, too, what the Resident would say when he heard she was leaving his prize patient, the former movie star.

But in spite of the man's former status, Kathy still failed to consider the case a plum. It had been hard work but oh, how very rewarding!

She heated the milk and prepared two chicken sandwiches, then added a fresh molasses cookie to the tray. "One of your cookies should put new life into the poor man," she told the cook, who had just taken a fresh pan from the oven. "If I weren't in a hurry, I should beg for one for Kathy Marshall as well," she added, as she slipped through the door.

The patient was watching for her return, his eyes eager, and Kathy warned him that he must eat slowly. "I snitched a fresh cookie for you, Mr. Amory," she told him. "We have a wonderful cook here at Memorial, and there's one thing that reminds me of home—the cookie jar is always full. I don't know how Mrs. Bunting manages it, but somehow she does. Good? ... You are a great credit to us, Mr. Amory," she told him, removing the tray. "How about a brief nap before dinner? I have an appointment with the Superintendent in about two minutes but will lower the shades and close your door."

"Don't be gone long, Kathy," the man begged, "and don't let them take you away from me."

The nurse smiled. "You won't need a special nurse much longer, Mr. Amory," she told him, "and really you aren't actually sick at all any more. Even a student nurse could take care of you from now on."

"I shall not remain here one minute after they take you off this case," he told her earnestly. "I'm used to you; you're used to me. We suit each other, and I'm willing to pay more if that is what is troubling the Superintendent. I mean it, Kathy. I won't let them take you away from me."

"I doubt if it is anything like that," Kathy reassured him. "It is probably something I have either done or left undone, some infringement of the strict rules. I don't know, but I'll find out right away. Be good while I'm gone, Mr. Amory, and I hope you can sleep. There. Comfortable?"

"Run along," he urged her, "and come right back. I may need you."

Kathy waved her hand to him and left. She had a feeling that she was not going to be allowed to leave this patient. He evidently had wealth, as well as prestige, and had the power to get what he wanted.

She walked down the three flights of stairs to the Superintendent's office and knocked lightly.

At the soft, "Come!" she entered and took the chair indicated. Miss Merriman looked almost severe, and Kathy felt a twinge as she thought quickly of what, if anything, she had done amiss.

She had not long to wait, however, for the Superintendent said evenly, "You have been a member of the Bostwick Memorial nursing staff for more than a year, have you not, Marshall?"

"A year the first of October, Miss Merriman," Kathy replied. "I came here immediately following my graduation from Hartwood Training School."

"I know. Then you must be aware of the rules governing the members of the staff of the average hospital—and this hospital in particular?"

"Of course," Kathy answered, her thought reverting to the threat made by Lois Bradley some weeks ago. She thought she had forgotten it, but now it came flooding back—the spitefulness in the older nurse's voice, the menace, and the threat conveyed. She waited for a moment.

The Superintendent appeared to hesitate as to the best manner of approach. Nurses were scarce, and she knew that none of them would accept criticism or reprimand easily. Kathy's gaze did not waver.

"It has come to my attention that you have, not once but many times, openly flaunted your complete disregard of these rules, Marshall," Miss Merriman said at last. Her voice was almost sad as she made the accusation, and Kathy stared at her in consternation.

"That is not true, Miss Merriman," she stated resentfully.

The Superintendent drew a notebook toward her and turned a page. "You were seen getting into a sleigh by several of the staff a few weeks ago—I haven't the exact date here, but it was during January, when sleighing was at its best. Dr. Elliott was driving. You returned just before midnight and were let into the nurses' annex by one of the older nurses. You were seen at Highland Park, skating with Dr. MacDonald and one of the interns—name not given. You were at the Riker Drugstore in company with another nurse and with the Resident, Dr. Channing. You were seen leaving a car recently, accompanied by Dr. Elliott; Dr. MacDonald was driving."

She paused. "These are the specific charges made against you, Marshall. Have you any explanation, any plausible explanation, for these infringements of the hospital rules? I want to be perfectly fair always, but I cannot and will not allow anything remotely resembling favoritism. That first infringement was perhaps my fault. In a weak moment I yielded to Dr. Elliott's plea for permission to take you sleigh riding. But the others, Marshall? Did you take advantage of that one concession and continue to break the rules?"

Kathy shook her head. She was close to tears, angry tears. "I had no date with Dr. MacDonald on the afternoon we were seen skating at Highland Park, Miss Merriman," she said stiffly. "After all, Bostwick is Dr. MacDonald's home town. I went alone, was there some time before he came, and left before he did. I skated a little with Dr. Matson, the intern mentioned, but he isn't a very good skater and I left and came back to the hospital alone. My friend, Irene Barker, and I stopped in at the drugstore one evening and bought coffee and chicken sandwiches, and while we were there Dr. Channing came in and joined us. I left him there and met Butch Adams outside and went over to see Dana. Peter brought me home, and he is certainly not a member of the staff. And last Saturday Dana invited some of us over for dinner because Peter was home for the week end. Peter came here for me and later, inasmuch as Dr. MacDonald had his car, he drove Dr. Elliott and me back to the hospital."

Her voice choked with anger.

"I fail to see where I have been so remiss in keeping the rules, Miss Merriman," she said, "and whoever reported these perfectly harmless and unexpected meetings to you was either maliciously mischievous or just plain spiteful. I have an idea who——" she broke off.

"I have done nothing of which to be ashamed, Miss Merriman," Kathy went on, more calmly, "and I refuse now to be treated as if I had."

She rose to her feet and prepared to leave the room.

"If I am to be dismissed," she added, "it will not be

89

because I plead guilty of any willful infringement of the hospital rules." Her head was high and her eyes very bright, and the Superintendent stood also.

"My dear girl," she said, and her voice was kind, "I never felt that you were guilty. A woman in my position soon learns to become more than a fair judge of human nature, and I have perfect confidence in most of my nurses and the staff in general. But you must realize that when charges are made it is my duty to weigh them thoroughly and to decide what is best to be done."

She hesitated. "You are young, Marshall," she went on, laying a gentle hand on the girl's shoulder, "and very, very lovely. You are an excellent nurse—willing, hard-working, and uncomplaining—and we in Bostwick Memorial love and admire you. You have enemies, of course. Who hasn't, that is outstanding? But let me quote the advice given me by a very wonderful man when in my youth I had been accused of currying favor. He said, 'Don't take it to heart, my dear, for they never knock a dead one.' I have thought of it often, and I pass it on to you for what it is worth. That is all, Marshall," she said and turned back to her desk. "I doubt if I shall hear any more about it. Thank you for coming so promptly."

Kathy left the room. She fought tears, whether of anger or hurt she didn't know. She only knew that she longed for a place where she could howl undisturbed. Instead, she hurried to the nearest washroom, bathed her hot cheeks and burning eyes in cold water, then went back to her patient and relaxed to find him sleeping quietly.

Outside, Bostwick was still experiencing its false spring. After all, it was only March now, but buds were large and bulbs were inches out of the ground. The branches of forsythia Kathy had brought in a week or more ago were now beginning to show definite signs of spilling sprays of gold into the hospital room. Was there a robin in that elm tree? She told herself it was really too early for robins, but she had already seen a flash of blue as a bird flew past her window yesterday. Yes, spring could not be far away, even if the calendar warned that there were still ten days of March to live through, March days with unpredictable weather and perhaps high winds.

She stood at the window, enjoying the warmth of the sun and the signs of promise spread out below her. Suddenly her dark mood lightened, and she smiled to herself that she could ever have allowed herself to become depressed. Not depressed when spring was so near; when her patient, once so very ill, was on the high road to complete recovery. Shame on her! After all, she said in her heart, "God's in His heaven—all's right with the world!" Her world anyway.

Dr. Elliott thrust his head in at the door and, seeing that her patient was sleeping, hissed softly and motioned her to join him in the corridor. Was this another infringement of the hospital rules? she wondered, then banished the thought. She must not allow herself to become unduly sensitive.

"I brought you a paper, Kathy?" he said softly. "Have you heard from any of the Adams family lately? No? Then you'll be interested in an editorial on the third page of the Bostwick *Dispatch*. Personally, I don't believe Butch was mixed up in the affair at all, but apparently there are others who do. I shall be glad when this job of yours is over. I've missed you. You work too hard. See you sometime," he added, and hurried away.

Kathy went back into the room and opened the paper to the third page. There it was.

VANDALISM AMONG OUR STUDENTS IN
ROGER BOSTWICK HIGH SCHOOL MUST STOP

"That the afternoon paper, Kathy?" David Amory asked. "May I have it when you are through with it?"

Kathy passed it to him. Butch Adams mixed up in vandalism? She did not believe it either.

Her patient spoke. "Young ruffians!" he muttered. "Every year a few hoodlums have to demonstrate their freedom from restraint by making idiots of themselves. They don't seem to care that they destroy property, destroy beauty, and lower the moral standards of their school by their behavior. They just try to outshine their predecessors, perhaps even their own fathers, in fiendish pranks. Too bad. Have you read the account here?"

Kathy shook her head. "I just this minute received the paper, but I happen to know one of the boys said to be involved, and I don't believe a word of it. Butch Adams wouldn't harm anyone or anything, Mr. Amory, and no one—not Mr. Blythe, the principal, himself or even the magistrate—can make me believe it."

David Amory's quick eye had scanned the editorial. "But young Adams wasn't mixed up in it until he went to the magistrate and confessed that he was with that group of boys. Apparently seven of the boys were rounded up and taken to police headquarters. Young Adams wasn't among them; he had gone home earlier. But he told the magistrate that he and members of an athletic team— basketball, it was—had gone over to the school with white- wash, to paint signs on the pavement along the road in front of the building. He said the words he painted were ROGER BOSTWICK HIGH BEAT ORDWELL. The signs ex- tended for perhaps a quarter of a mile each way. He said he had no idea there was anything else done until later, when he heard of the arrests and that the façade had been splashed with whitewash too. But, he had insisted, he was with the fellows and so supposed he was as guilty as they. Of course he was in a way," Amory murmured, "but do you know, Kathy? I admire that youngster, although prob- ably the others would have involved him anyway. So you know the lad?"

"I know the family, Mr. Amory," Kathy said, "and they are fine. Butch hasn't a mean streak in his make-up. I be- lieve I shall go over there tonight when I get off duty."

"I doubt if the authorities will do anything about it, Kathy," the man said comfortingly. "Most men, if they told the truth, have done something of the sort during high school or college days. Perhaps they will have to pay for the cleaning, or be made to do it themselves, which would be punishment enough, I'm sure. I shall be inter- ested in hearing young Adams' handling of the affair."

"I'll know more about it when I've seen him," she told him. "Do you suppose they will lock them up in jail, Mr. Amory? I know they haven't much money—Butch and his family, I mean—for bail, you know."

David Amory laughed. "I doubt if they will even be charged with malicious mischief, Kathy," he told her. "After all, men were once boys, you know, and even a magistrate can be human. Don't worry."

But Kathy did worry, and later when she met Dr. El- liott in the corridor she asked him what he thought of it and what he thought the punishment would be. He shrugged and said he doubted if anything would be done at all. "But the young rascals should be made to clean up the mess. Do 'em good,' he said, "although I guess we all go through that smart-aleck stage of wanting to break the law and destroy things. It's part of growing up, I suppose."

Kathy didn't agree, but she started for the Adams home with a lighter heart because Dr. Elliott had dismissed the subject so easily. She had seen little of the Adams family lately, partly because of her long working hours and partly because Irene Barker and she had been busy preparing for the annual bazaar and dance to be held soon after Easter. But she had talked with Dana from time to time and rejoiced with her that even the persistent limp in her walk had almost disappeared. It would be good to see them all again.

CHAPTER ELEVEN

BUTCH ADAMS OPENED THE DOOR, in answer to Kathy Marshall's ring, and grinned when he recognized her.

"Don't look so all-fired serious, Kathy," he greeted her. "The very worst they can do is make us scrub the front of the building, but I don't imagine the prank will be punished at all. The dads of some of the fellows have influence—big taxpayers, stand well in the community, and all that sort of thing. Of course I'm not lucky that way, but I'm quite able and willing to take my medicine, whatever they dish out to us." He spoke with bravado, and Kathy wondered if it was for the family's benefit.

"But, Butch, you weren't actually involved," she said earnestly. "It isn't at all like you. I couldn't believe it, and no one who knows you will believe it."

"Thanks, Kathy," he murmured. "The thing is, though, that not everyone in Bostwick knows of my unimpeachable character." He grinned wryly. "Least of all the police, and the magistrate wasn't too impressed with my gesture of aligning myself with the other guys. Probably though I was playing to the grandstand, making a good fellow of myself." He sighed and his face flushed, probably at some unpleasant memory.

"I don't care what they think or what anyone says, Butch," the girl said stoutly. "We who know you believe you did a brave and decent thing and admire you for it. Is there anything I can do to help?"

Butch put his arm around her and led her into the

living room, where his sister and grandmother were sitting. "See what I found on our front doorstep, folks," he told them. "Bad news travels fast, you see, and so here came our Kathy to the rescue. Only——"

"Darling!" cried Dana, rushing to her. "How sweet of you to come! Gram has been much more worried than I. They can't do anything to Butch, can they, Kathy?" she asked doubtfully. "He isn't a hoodlum."

"Of course not. No one who knows him will believe that. We all think it was proved without doubt when of his own free will he went to the magistrate and confessed to being one of the group who were later arrested. I doubt if many boys would have had the integrity to do it. I'm proud of him, Mrs. Hammond," she went on, sitting down.

Martha Hammond was knitting steadily and silently, her usually serene face troubled. Now she smiled at the visitor and laid a hand on hers as it rested on the couch between them. "Thank you, my dear," she murmured.

"Gram doesn't approve of me, Kathy," Butch said dolefully, and the girl knew he was hurt.

"I am merely disappointed, Butch," his grandmother said softly.

"Well, I'm not," his sister was quick to add. "What else could he have done, Gram?" she demanded. "Let the others take the rap just because he happened to come home early? And what would the other fellows have thought of him then? No, darling, I feel sure Butch did the right thing, and someday others will realize it, too. You just wait and see."

"I'm quite willing to wait, Dana," Mrs. Hammond told her.

The doorbell sounded and Butch, who was nearest, went to answer the summons. The three in the living room heard a low-voiced conversation, and then Dr. Mac-Donald entered the room.

"Why the doldrums?" he asked, as he took the chair Butch placed for him. "Don't tell me you are worried about that high school affair, Mrs. Hammond. Didn't Pete ever get into scrapes?"

"Never!" It was Butch who answered. "Peter was all Gram hoped and prayed for, Doc. I guess I've always been something of a black sheep—a problem child—to Gram. Poor Gram!" He sighed sadly.

94

"You're nothing of the sort, and you know it," his grandmother denied. "But to have his name—the Adams name—dragged through the courts, printed in the papers, called a hoodlum—my grandson! Where could I have failed?"

Butch flung himself to his knees before her and gathered her into his arms. "Gram, Gram!" he cried. "You never failed. I tell you I didn't do a thing wrong. I told the magistrate and you the whole truth, but I couldn't let the other kids take what punishment there might be without doing what I could for them. You wouldn't want me to act the coward, Gram. Don't you see what would have happened? It would surely have leaked out that I had been with that gang and had left them to take the rap. Don't shake your head, Gram. I know people, and I know I did the right thing, and they—the police, the magistrate, and Mr. Blythe himself, too—can think what they've a mind to. I can take my medicine, Gram," he added, and buried his face in her lap, where the old lady tousled his curly hair and patted his cheek.

Butch got to his feet then, winked at the doctor, and grinned wryly at Kathy. Mrs. Hammond looked relieved, and Kathy felt sure that her youngest grandchild knew how to handle her. She rose to leave.

"Don't go, Kathy," Dana begged, but Kathy felt sure there was no real urgency in the plea. Wasn't Dr. MacDonald here? So she insisted that she must get back to the hospital. Gary MacDonald offered to drive her back, but she shook her head.

"Don't bother," she told him, and saw the relief in Dana's face. "The bus runs right past the hospital, and I can get one at the end of your street here. And you don't have to come either, Butch," she laughed, as the boy started for the hall closet and his coat. "It's not late, and I'm not in the least afraid. Don't be silly. Oh, well," she ended, as he came to the door, drawing on his gloves but hatless as usual. She made her farewells and saw with relief that the air of the room was considerably lighter.

"Are you too tired to walk to the terminal, Kathy?" Butch wanted to know, as they reached the street. "You can board a bus there and won't have to change. I don't get to see you often, you know."

"No," Kathy told him, "I'm not at all tired. As it happens I have been on a case lately that requires very little attention. At first it was pretty hard, but Mr. Amory is recovering nicely."

"I know," the boy said. "I read all about Amory, once America's greatest lover, being at death's door. But I didn't know until just last week that he was here in Bostwick Memorial. Haven't lost your heart to him, have you, Kathy?" he asked.

"Of course not," the nurse told him emphatically. "He's very nice, very kind and cooperative, but it is hard to believe he was ever a motion picture star. Of course he is beginning to look better—adding a little weight and getting more color—but it will be some time before he will look the part to me."

"Did you notice that Dana is walking all right, or nearly all right, Kathy?" he asked. "If it wasn't for Gram I bet she would be going back to work most any day. Of course none of us want her to, but Dana loves her job and—well, she feels she can use the money although the firm has been paying her a part of her salary ever since she has been out. Maybe that's why she feels she should go back as soon as she can. The Adams integrity, you know."

"I know," Kathy agreed, "and, Butch, that is a very wonderful attribute."

"I wasn't bragging," the boy apologized. "I was just joking."

"But it's true," the girl told him, "and something for which to be proud."

"Do you like Doc, Kathy? I mean Gary MacDonald?"

"Yes," Kathy answered. She felt the hot blood in her face and was glad of the dark. "I think he is a fine doctor —surgeon—and a fine man. Why?"

"Oh, nothing," the boy answered. "Gram likes him, and I guess Sis has fallen pretty hard for him. I don't know about him, though." They crossed the street and walked on toward the terminal.

"Dana's sweet," Kathy said, wondering just why it was that even the mention of Dr. MacDonald's name should bring a blush to her cheeks. She felt sure that while she liked him she didn't love him. In fact she had come to admire Bill Elliott more. Her thoughts reverted to the recent talk with the Superintendent. There must be no more compromising situations involving her with any of the male members of the staff. She sighed deeply, and Butch stared down at her.

"What's wrong, Kathy?" he asked. "What did that prodigious sigh mean? Are you getting tired? I forget that you are on your feet most of the day.

Kathy laughed. "Don't be silly," she told him. "I was just thinking of something that happened this afternoon."

"Unpleasant, of course, from the size of that sigh. Why do you stick to nursing, Kathy?" he asked. "How can you stand some of the complaints, moanings, and sufferings of people? I should think it would drive you nuts."

"It doesn't," the girl replied. "We are trained to meet everything with which we come in contact with calmness, fortitude, and infinite patience. Sympathy, too, but not too pronounced, just in our care of the suffering. Too much sympathy can be bad for some people, you know. Sometimes it isn't easy, Butch, but who expects their work, or life itself, to be easy for them? There are days and nights when we wonder just why we chose to become nurses, but those occasions are rare. Most nurses love their work, love taking care of the sick, and grow stronger and more competent as time goes on. I'm a much better nurse now than I was when I first entered Memorial. Experience may be a hard teacher but it is a good one, a thorough one. We learn by practice. I know that."

Butch laughed somewhat ruefully. "That sounds funny coming from a kid like you, Kathy. Oh, I know your great age. You can't fool me, though. I know you are a mere infant in some things in spite of your experience with life and death. But I love listening to you. You do me good. By the way, how's the queen's favorite at present?"

"Queen's favorite, Butch?" Kathy asked puzzled at the question. "What do you mean?"

"Elliott, Doc Elliott," he elaborated.

Kathy laughed. "And I'm supposed to be the queen, is that it? You're funny, Butch. Bill Elliott is a fine man. I like him. As far as I know, he's all right. He was when I left the hospital. I met him in the corridor, in fact it was he who brought me the paper containing the news of your —shall we say *beau geste?* And listen, Butch, he told me not to worry about you because it was just a part of growing up, and that all boys did something of the sort at the time of their adolescence. It sort of comforted me."

"I like his nerve," the boy growled. "Adolescence, indeed. I'll have him know I'm no adolescent. I'm a man, though not yet in my dotage as he probably is."

"Poor Butch!" Kathy laughed, as they drew near to the terminal. "I'm sure Dr. Elliott had no thought of insulting you. He's fond of you and told me he admired you and your whole family."

"Just the same," Butch began, then caught her hand in his and hurried her to the waiting bus. "I'm coming over to get you some evening," he promised, "and we'll take in a movie or dine and dance somewhere. And tell that Elliott for me that he'd better be careful who he calls an adolescent. Goodbye."

Kathy smiled to herself. Of course Butch was an adolescent, and what was so insulting about that?

The bus rolled along, stopping from time to time to take on or let off passengers, and at last began the long climb to Memorial Hospital, where it stopped to let Kathy off and to take on some dozen new passengers, evidently visitors at the hospital. Nine o'clock. Nearly everyone left at that time, and as Kathy mounted the two wide steps to the walk leading to the front entrance she met several others who greeted her pleasantly without stopping. Evidently they, too, were hoping to catch a bus back to town.

She swerved before reaching the porch and walked rapidly around the building to the nurses' annex some distance in the rear. She was suddenly tired; she felt the need of a bath and perhaps a glass of warm milk. She stopped in the kitchen, but found it empty, and mounted the stairs to her room, hoping no one was there.

"Well, and where have you been all evening, Kathy Marshall?" a cheerful voice greeted her. "I've been sitting here waiting for hours. What happened? Heavy date?"

Kathy shook her head. "Did you read the afternoon paper, Irene?" she asked, and, as the other shook her head, she went on, "Well, some of the high school boys got mixed up in a rather disastrous prank and Butch Adams, while not actually involved, was roped into it. I went over to see if I could do anything to help. I know how his grandmother adores all those children, and I was afraid she might be upset."

Irene Barker hooted derisively. "Little Miss Fix-it!

98

Why don't you mind your own business? And was the old lady upset? Probably it wasn't the first time one of her grandchildren has managed to get involved, as you say, in mischief."

"She took it very hard, Irene," Kathy told her, as she hung up her coat. "But everyone else seems to think there is little chance of actual trouble over the affair. I hope not for her sake."

"What did the young hellions do, for heaven's sake?"

"Smeared whitewash over the front of the classic school —quite thoroughly, from the account."

"Don't worry, Kathy," Irene told her cynically. "Bostwick taxpayers will come across. Boys will be boys, you know, or words to that effect. If one of them were my son he'd get his jacket warmed, and don't you forget it. They should be made to clean up the whole mess while a policeman stands over them to see it's done right. Honestly, Kathy, kids seem to get more obsteperous each generation, only they call it delinquency nowadays. Whose delinquency?"

Kathy laughed without mirth. "You just think so, Irene," she said. "Most of it is plain youthful exuberance —animal spirits. I have it from a man who professes to know about such things."

"Who?"

"My patient, David Amory, ex-movie star, ex-great-lover, and soon ex-patient, I hope. Really, Irene, the man has shown a remarkable vitality and will to live when everything was against him. Do you remember him at all?"

"Sure I remember him. He was once my ideal, as he was the ideal of most of the girls of my time. Didn't you ever hear of him?" As Kathy shook her head, she went on, "Such is fame. How does he look? Handsome? Attractive?"

"Neither," the younger nurse said. "He's improving, but he's still thin and haggard, though I'll say this for him, he has the sweetest disposition in the world. And he never talks about himself, of his glamorous past or the lovely ladies who pursued him. No one comes to see him. He gets no mail, and the only flowers that have come for him are from the wife of his doctor, who sent him here. Certainly he isn't running true to form, is he?"

99

Irene Barker pursed her lips for a moment then said determinedly, "I intend having urgent business with you tomorrow afternoon while you are on duty, my girl." She laughed impishly. "I want to see for myself just how much of what you say about him is true. I shall profess to have been one of his most ardent fans in the dear dead past, Kathy. Is he able to be up yet?"

Kathy shook her head. "Not out of bed. I pile pillows behind him, and he sits up for a while each day. I don't think you should come, Irene. After all, perhaps he is sensitive about his appearance."

"Pooh!" Irene scoffed. "Men aren't sensitive like that. And they like attention—eat it up. You'll see."

"Just the same, I wish you would talk to Dr. Channing before you come," Kathy told her. "After all, he has had no visitors, not one since he has been here. I thought it was strange at first, but the Resident assured me it was the way he wanted it. No callers, no mail, no telephone calls, and that's the way it has been for five solid weeks. You talk to Channing before you decide. I should dislike having to refuse you entrance, Irene, but orders are orders, and I'm on duty and responsible, you know."

"Oh, have it your own way," the older nurse said peevishly. "After all, he's nothing in my young life. Let him perish of loneliness, for all I care."

"Don't be like that, Irene," Kathy murmured.

"Forget it," the other said sharply. "Have you heard anything about some of the girls being called on the carpet because of rules infringements? I heard one of the nurses over in Pediatrics declare that Annie had better not say anything to her or she would shake the dust of Bostwick Memorial from her feet in short order. Have you heard anything about it?"

Kathy bit her lip. "Oh yes," she replied. "One of the nurses took it upon herself to report me to the Superintendent."

"Report you?" Irene cried in astonishment. "Who was it, and what did she say? Tell me at once." Irene was angry. She hated tattlers and had always felt that Memorial was exceptionally free from such things. "Why wasn't I told before?" she demanded irately.

"It just happened this afternoon," Kathy said, "and I was as much surprised as you are. But it seems that someone has been snooping on my activities and has turned in my perfectly innocent meetings with one or two of the doctors at various times. Listen, even that chance meeting you and I had with Channing was reported, but your name was not mentioned. Just mine."

"Of all the filthy tricks!" Irene cried. "What did Annie say to you?"

"Not much. She listed my misdemeanors and asked for excuses, if any. I explained every single instance. I have certainly kept the rules here, and I told her so. She believed me and told me she hadn't thought me guilty from the first, but the charges had been made and it was her duty to investigate them."

"It was her duty to discharge the talebearer," Irene declared hotly. "Did she tell you who made the report, Kathy?"

"She didn't have to."

"Why, do you know? Who was it? I insist upon knowing. No one is safe with a troublemaker running around loose."

Kathy snapped her fingers to show her complete indifference to anything the person could do. "I am not going to tell you, Irene," she said. "I wouldn't give her the satisfaction of thinking she alarmed me. I intend to ignore it and shall treat her as I always have—pleasantly. Do you know, Irene, Miss Merriman gave me a pretty good slogan to live by, and I'll pass it on to you. She said that a very wonderful man told her once, when she had been accused of currying favor, to remember, 'They never knock a dead one.' Good? I think so. Now I wonder if it would be possible to get a glass of warm milk and a sandwich here. I went out without my dinner, and evidently the Adams family had already dined when I arrived. I didn't stay very long, anyway."

"I'll get you some milk and a sandwich, Kathy," her friend offered. "I'm sure Mrs. Bunting will let me have it, and if she isn't there I shall help myself and leave a note. I've done it before, and she said it was all right. Be back in a jiffy, darling. Get into a robe and slippers and relax."

The door closed behind her, and Kathy followed the advice. The bath could wait. It wasn't any too warm here just now, and the woolly robe and fur-lined slippers felt comfortable. When the older nurse returned she was fast asleep in her chair, but roused long enough to dispose of the food and drink her friend had brought to her. Irene didn't linger. She saw that the younger nurse was exhausted and left within a few minutes. Kathy undressed and got into bed, to fall asleep almost instantly.

CHAPTER TWELVE

MARCH HURRIED ALONG on its more or less tempestuous way, quieted down long enough to leave like the proverbial lamb, and it was April! Robins were back in force, and an occasional bluebird flashed brightly across the watcher's gaze to lift sagging spirits with the promise of better days to come. The wary weatherman still warned of a fool's paradise—that, after all, the season was early and there was plenty of time yet for snow—but no one would believe him. The snow was gone, wasn't it? Trees showed bursting buds, bulbs were definitely shedding their winter covering, and the air was soft and mild. Most of the patients in Bostwick Memorial sensed the change and reacted accordingly. There were a few disgruntled souls who agreed with the weatherman's prediction that things were not what they seemed and that cold weather, even a blizzard or two, was entirely possible.

David Amory was out of bed for the greater part of each day now, and while he still remained aloof to visitors he insisted that Kathy Marshall be retained as his nurse during his waking hours. The Chief of Staff didn't approve of catering to a patient's demands, but in this case he had little or nothing to say. Miss Merriman was the one who voiced the most objections. Marshall was one of her best, most dependable nurses, and should not be subjected to such long hours. Why, there was even a chance of a normal complaint being made by the Board of Managers, all of whom stressed the necessity of adhering closely to the state law of eight-hour duty. But after expressing her views to the patient, she withdrew her objections—that is, she was no longer openly opposed to Kathy's remaining as his special.

Kathy laughed at the man's smug expression when the door closed on the Superintendent of Nurses. "I suppose that was an example of the famous Amory charm," she teased. "You're actually dangerous," she added.

The man grinned. "I don't know about the charm, Kathy," he replied, "but it's the method I use when I want my own way. It invariable works, too. My stay here isn't going to be much longer, and I couldn't endure getting used to another nurse. Did I ever tell you how very wonderful you are, my dear? You are an unusual nurse. What a wife you are going to make for some lucky man! I wish I were twenty, or even ten, years younger, and I should give him a run for his money. But I'm too old, just the patched-up wreck of a man. Is it Elliott, Kathy? Or is it none of my business?" As the girl shook her head and bit her lip in embarrassment, he went on, "Not the Resident, Kathy, not Channing. He's nearly as old as I am, and you need youth. Better settle for Elliott. He's good, he's right, and I'm sure he is in love with you. Don't shake your head at me, Miss Marshall," he laughed. "I'm something of a wizard, they tell me."

"Who are 'they'?" the girl asked. "Dr. Elliott and I are good friends and staff members. I like him, that's all." She spoke almost impatiently. Why was it that if a nurse and a doctor seem to be friendly, everyone thought that it must be love? "They" made her sick. How annoyed and embarrassed Bill Elliott would be if any of this talk got back to him.

"What are you ruminating over, Kathy?" the patient wanted to know. "Don't tell me that you are annoyed at my bluntness. I wouldn't hurt you for the world, and you should know it by this time. Have you ever considered entering the moving picture industry? I know most girls have at one time or another, but have you?"

"Never!" Kathy said emphatically. "I never even wanted to become an actress, which I am aware is not at all natural. But I always wanted to become a nurse and devote my life to caring for the sick and unfortunate. I even planned to go into welfare work—do public health in the slums of New York's East Side—but my people talked me out of that. I had a hard enough time gaining their consent to entering a nurses' training school, but in that I was determined. I'm very careful when I write home never to tell of the hardships and the many disagreeable duties with which a nurse has to cope in an average day's work. I make my letters as interesting and glamorous as possible, and truly, some of it is both, so why stress the other?"

103

"And that, Kathy Marshall, is the way to meet one's daily life," the man said approvingly. "That has always been my philosophy. And in spite of the years of invalidism that has been my portion, life has been good to me. Perhaps I shall never again take up my old line of work—perhaps that door is closed definitely—but I believe that when one door closes another miraculously opens, if we have eyes and heart to see."

"You're nice, Mr. Amory," the nurse told him. "It has been a joy taking care of you. The only thing is that now when I have a really hard case I may find it difficult to handle it. You have spoiled me."

"No danger—ah, good morning, Doctor," he greeted the Resident. "Lovely morning!"

"It is," the Resident replied, "and we are going to take you for a stroll down the corridor to the east solarium and let the good old sun give you one of her famous treatments. Game for it?"

"I haven't done much walking," the man demurred, "and I dislike asking Miss Marshall to act as a crutch. Could one of the orderlies give me an arm, Doctor?"

"Of course. I doubt if Marshall would be much good to you in your present condition. I'm going to take your weight, Amory," he went on. "I'm willing to wager that you are within twenty pounds of your normal weight."

"One hundred seventy? Oh no, not within fifty pounds. Why, I feel actually a featherweight. Willing to put up something on that, Doc?" He grinned. "We'll let Kathy, here, hold the money. You say twenty, I say fifty. What is your opinion, Nurse?" he asked.

Kathy looked dubious. "I'm not much good at guessing either ages or weights," she told them judicially, "but offhand I should say you weighed around a hundred thirty-five or forty-five."

"O.K., lead me to the scales, Doctor." The patient laughed, getting shakily to his feet. "Where's that orderly? Oh, hello, there! How's your muscle this morning? Give me your arm, Nurse," he murmured, "and let's go. You come along too, Doc, and we'll settle this matter now."

The small procession left the room and slowly made its way along the long corridor to the solarium. It was a long walk for the invalid, and when he reached a chair he was trembling and his face was damp with perspiration. But he was inordinately proud of his ability.

"Rest awhile and then we'll tackle that weight problem," the Resident told him, dismissing the orderly for the moment. "Relax, man, and enjoy this wonderful sunshine. Spring is here. See that robin already building his home and making it waterproof and weatherproof? All right, now. Ready for the few steps to the scales? I doubt if you will need help this time, but if you do, Marshall and I will be right here. Come on. Remember that bet, and by the way what were the stakes? Candy? Pooh, that's no bet. Make it a five-spot. O.K.? Here you are."

The man had reached the scales and stood uncertainly for a moment, while Dr. Channing put a sustaining hand at his elbow. Then he lifted himself to the scales. For a moment Kathy feared he would topple, but he steadied and asked jubilantly, "How much? No fair adding one of your own feet, Doc. Kathy, you look. How much?"

Both the Resident and the nurse bent over the small weighing machine and cried in unison, "140 pounds! Who wins?"

"You see, Doctor?" the patient pointed out. "I'm still thirty pounds below my normal weight but twenty pounds heavier than I thought. So, I think my nurse, here, who came closest, should have the five. Do you happen to have that amount on you, Doc? My wallet's in my other pants."

Dr. Channing handed Kathy a five-dollar bill and shook his head at the patient. "I believe the beggar intended to fleece me all the time. The man's dangerous."

Kathy slipped the bill into her pocket, determined to return it to the Resident when they met outside. But it had been fun, and the patient was relaxed and cheerful, so the experiment had been successful. She moved his chair into the direct rays of the warm April sun and spread a rug across his knees.

"An hour of this will do wonders for you, Mr. Amory," she told him, when the Resident had left the room. "Perhaps you might even doze, but with such a wonderful view I doubt if you will. Do you want reading matter or something to eat right now?"

"Nothing, Kathy," the man answered. "You have no idea what this has done for me. Now, for the first time, I feel sure of my ultimate recovery."

105

"I never had any doubt of it," the nurse said. "After all, you have responded wonderfully to the treatment given you, and constitutionally you are sound. Another week or so should find you well enough to leave the hospital and take up your life where you left it so many months—or is it years?—ago."

"I suppose this disease got started long ago," he said musingly, "but I was too busy or too indifferent to take time out for a physical examination and possible hospitalization. Foolish, I grant you, but after all, I have enjoyed being here—with you."

"How about visitors, Mr. Amory?" Kathy asked, after a moment.

The man hesitated. "I don't know," he murmured. "I suppose there is a stack of mail waiting until I give the signal that I am going to live. My secretary does exceptionally well in handling such things, but I'm sure he will be relieved to hear from me. Could you get me a pad of telegraph blanks, Kathy? That's the easiest method of announcing my resurrection, I suppose. Where's that orderly? I want to go back to my room. I can't concentrate here."

"There!" he said, almost regretfully. "The die is cast. I am definitely among the living once more. Henceforth the peace and tranquillity that has been my portion, these weeks past, is no more. And do you know, Kathy Marshall?" he went on apprehensively. "I'm almost afraid. I have discovered I don't care for the average person any more."

"I wish you would see a dear friend of mine, Mr. Amory," Kathy said impulsively. "She is one of your former fans. She is a little older than I am and remembers you when you were indeed the great lover. I haven't let her visit you before, even though she has begged me to let her come. How about it? How about meeting one of the loveliest, sweetest nurses here in Memorial? I'm sure you both should enjoy knowing each other. Shall I tell her you will see her this afternoon?"

The frown that had settled on the man's face for a moment was quickly dispelled, and his most winning smile appeared. "Anyone who can remember me fondly for all those years should have my deepest gratitude, Kathy. I should enjoy meeting a friend of yours. There is

106

someone else I should like to meet also, while I am here, if you can manage it. The Adams boy—Butch, I think you called him."

"You would enjoy Dana, his sister, too," Kathy assured him. "I'll put in a call and have them come this afternoon if possible. I think Dana has gone back to work. She has been planning to ever since she made that trip upstairs. She is the girl who broke her hip last fall and made such a wonderful recovery. They should come soon, for I imagine your telegrams are going to bring a flood of responses—visits, flowers, letters, gifts, and all that sort of thing. To quote someone or other, 'For this our king was dead and is alive again.' We here at Memorial are all as happy as you are over your recovery, Mr. Amory, and I'm going to miss you."

"You're sweet, Kathy Marshall," the man said gently, "and I expect to miss you and your patient and devoted care for the remainder of my life. If at any time I can do anything for you, anything at all, will you promise me to let me do it? I am at your service now and as long as I shall live."

Kathy's smile was tremulous. She had grown fond of this charming and unexacting patient. "That is a large promise, Mr. Amory," she told him. "As long as you live. I hope it will prove a long, happy, and full life. Now before I become sentimental I shall do a bit of telephoning. And your lunch will be arriving soon. Please be careful. Eat slowly, and if you want anything changed or would like more of something, don't hesitate to make your wants known. I have never felt really satisfied since I turned over the preparing of your tray to the dietitian instead of taking care of it myself. But Johnson, our chief dietitian, never did approve of my continuing to prepare your tray instead of letting her take care of it as she did the other special cases. You see, Mr. Amory, there is such a thing as professional pride even among hospital staff members, and Johnson is a fine dietitian."

The man laughed. "I know, Kathy," he told her, "and I shall be careful, chew every bite, never drink when my mouth is full of food, and give Johnson the devil if I don't like the contents of her tray. There, is that satisfactory? Run along, my dear, and break the glad news to your friends that I shall be at home all afternoon. Get hold of that orderly before you go, and tell him I want a shave and a haircut. I've discovered he's an extra special barber among his other accomplishments. Don't be gone long. I miss you if you're not where I can see you. Good-by, and don't forget the orderly."

Kathy called the Adams home, and Mrs. Hammond answered. She was sure both Dana and Butch would be thrilled to call on Mr. Amory. "And," she added, laughing, "maybe I shall come with them. I, too, have pleasant recollections of him. My husband was an ardent admirer of him and his work, and when a mere man speaks glowingly of an actor—especially one bearing the title of 'The Great Lover'— I'm sure he must have worth-while attributes. So if it will be all right, I believe I shall accompany my grandchildren. About five-thirty? That will suit us beautifully, and thank you, my dear, for thinking of us."

"How is Dana these days? And the job? Is she experiencing any difficulty in getting about?"

"None at all, Kathy. She vows she will dance at your Easter party. Dr. MacDonald has already invited her, and she has been doing a great deal of practicing during the past week or so. It is really remarkable, the progress she has made. We had a time getting her to go down to the basement at first, but now she seems to have completely lost any fear she had regarding the place. We are all so happy about it."

"And we here at Memorial are too, Mrs. Hammond, and I shall expect you and the others at five-thirty this afternoon."

"How's tricks, Marshall?" he asked, pausing beside her. "I understand from the flood of telegrams our star patient just released that Memorial is in for an onslaught of notables. The question is whether or not we can stand it."

"Not us, Doctor," Kathy assured him, "but do you suppose Mr. Amory can stand it? He's having his first small dose of visitors this afternoon. First Irene Barker, and later some of the Adams family. I wouldn't be at all surprised if, as the news leaks out, more of the townspeople storms our gates for a glimpse of him. Fame is a wonderful thing, isn't it?"

The Resident said musingly, "Yes, I suppose it is, but

it is a flimsy and fleeting thing to bank on. Neither Amory nor we know how the recipients of those wires are going to take the news of his recovery. After all, he has been out of public life a decade, and people have a way of forgetting. Sometimes we find the trait admirable, and at other times forgetfulness can be a great blow to one's pride. I'm glad he is to have a few callers today. I know Barker was peeved at me because I objected to her visit weeks ago, but I was sure the man wasn't ready for visitors, even so charming a one. I'll see you later, and then we'll know how he stands the ordeal."

When Kathy returned to her patient some half hour later, she found him shaved, barbered, and fully dressed as if for the street in a gray tweed suit, white shirt, blue tie with a matching handkerchief in his breast pocket, socks of the same shade of blue, and comfortable and expensive-looking oxfords.

The nurse paused in the doorway to exclaim, "I should never have known you. You—you look wonderful! But better not be too ambitious, Mr. Amory. Remember you haven't been long out of bed. Why did you get dressed? It would have been all right to receive your callers in pajamas and dressing gown. After all, this is a hospital, and you have been a very sick man. Don't be so proud. I want you to know that I don't approve of you." She spoke severely, and the man stared in astonishment.

"Why, Kathy," he chided. "I thought you would be pleased. The orderly helped me. I didn't do too much—couldn't, as a matter of cold fact—but I wanted you to be proud of me." His face was clouded and the nurse, while disapproving the unnecessary exertion he must have expended, didn't have the heart to continue her rebuke. She wondered what Dr. Channing would say, but decided to make the best of it and wait.

"Did you have a satisfactory lunch?" she asked, after a moment.

"I had all I wanted," the man said, "but I didn't enjoy it as I would if you had been here with me. However, I obeyed your orders. Don't I look all right?"

"You look wonderful," she told him again, "but right now you are going to take a nap. Your first caller won't appear until three or a little after, so you can sleep for an hour. And," she told him sternly, "see that you do."

"Yes, Nurse," he said meekly, and Kathy lowered the shades and drew a light blanket across his knees. He caught her hand for a moment and asked contritely, "You're not really angry with me?"

Kathy smiled at him, and he raised her hand to his lips, then let it drop, and closed his eyes. Kathy left the room, closing the door behind her. Poor chap, she told herself, as she went back to the telephone for another try for her friend, sickness makes infants of the bravest and strongest of men.

CHAPTER THIRTEEN

IRENE BARKER was almost shy when she entered room 411A that afternoon, but the man in the chair by the window rose slowly to his feet and greeted her warmly.

"I can quite understand Kathy's enthusiasm for her closest friend, Miss Barker," he told her. "It is kind of you to remember me, although I doubt if it is so much actual memory as newspaper gossip. You must have been very young at the time of my greatest so-called fame. Anyway, I am happy to meet a friend of Kathy's, to whom I owe so very much. Sit down, my dear, and talk to me. Do you know you are my very first visitor? A dubious honor, perhaps, but one I appreciate. I hope it augurs well for the future. My world has slipped away from me, and I have been almost fearful of re-entering it. You have given me courage."

His manner was so kind, so easy and friendly, that Irene relaxed and was soon chattering in her normal whimsical manner, and Kathy saw that the man was having a very good time. His laugh rang out from time to time, and Irene remained until Mrs. Hammond arrived with Butch and Dana. They, too, appeared somewhat diffident at first. After all, David Amory's name was still one to demand respect and admiration. He called himself a has-been, but to those who remembered him he was not and never would be entirely forgotten.

Now he greeted the newcomers with pleasure, while Irene Barker slipped from the room. Mrs. Hammond told of her late husband's admiration for his ability, while Butch gazed at him with frank interest.

"You are all so kind," David Amory told them. "My entire stay here in Bostwick has been memorable. I shall

110

never forget you, any of you. And you have every right to be proud of your grandson, Mrs. Hammond," he said, smiling at the boy. "I have been anxious to meet him." He held out his hand to Butch, who grasped it closely. "I was just such a teen-ager once, Mrs. Hammond," he added. "At least I like to think that, even though I was undoubtedly mischievous and got into all sorts of trouble, there was honesty, bravery, and integrity back of it that prevented me from resorting to meanness or ugliness in any form. What do you plan to make of your life, Butch?" he asked.

"Oh, I want to be an engineer," the boy answered promptly. "But"—he frowned—"I'm not too hot in math. I enjoy chem, but math sort of eludes me, and of course I have to have math to become any kind of an engineer. I get by, of course," he went on dubiously, "but it's a tough hurdle, and I may flunk the finals, "Now, Gram"—he grinned at his disturbed grandmother—"I haven't flunked 'em yet, so don't look so disapproving."

The man sitting before them laughed. "Don't worry too much about it, Butch," he said. "No doubt you'll get through all right. I, myself, was none too good in mathematics either. English, Latin, French—languages were easy for me, but math, as you call it, was beyond me. However, I managed school and the university all right, and somehow math took its place among the 'alsos' in the curriculum."

"When did you decide to become an actor, Mr. Amory?" Butch wanted to know.

"I don't recall that I ever really decided it, Butch," he said. "I seem to have just drifted into it. I acted in college, played—for fun— in one or two Little Theater groups, and was offered a job on a picture they were casting in Hollywood. I must have clicked, for I stayed on, until ten years ago when my health let me down and I was forced to take a very long vacation. I doubt if I shall ever return to the stage now. From now on I intend to *live* life, not act a part. This invalidism has taught me a great deal, my friends," he added, almost apologetically. "I sound like an exhorter of some kind, don't I?"

"I like it," Butch told him. "And I'm glad to know someone else who was no wizard in math. I hope someday I, too, shall be a success in whatever job I have to do.

You see, I've got to make Gram proud of me. It will probably be tough going, but I've simply got to do it."

Mrs. Hammond laughed gently. "Poor Butch!" she said. "I imagine I have been a bit harsh with him at times."

"I decided right then to be an actor, Mr. Amory," he said, "and I was already dedicated to medicine. Consecrated, I should have said, because, you see, my father was a doctor, and Mother and I felt I should take up the work where an untimely death compelled Father to drop it. I only hope I shall become as good a man, doctor, and surgeon as he was," he added simply.

Mrs. Hammond nodded her approval, but Dana frowned, and Kathy wondered why. Something must have happened to annoy her, for she looked quite unimpressed by her doctor's confession of faith.

"What is this, anyway?" she asked coolly. "An experience meeting? Testimony, I think they call it in church, don't they? Now, Kathy, give your testimony, if any."

The nurse was startled. For the first time she wondered if her friend had become spoiled from so much attention. It didn't sound at all like the Dana she loved. She saw Gary MacDonald flush, his mother's eyes widen in astonishment, and Mrs. Hammond shake her head at her granddaughter.

"Oh, mine isn't at all interesting," she said quickly, hoping to ease the sudden tension. "I just wanted to become a nurse and I became one. Short and to the point. How about yourself, Dana? What have you to contribute?"

"Sis got out of bed from the wrong side this morning," Butch said to no one in particular. "I told her she was getting to be a spoiled brat, and she resented it." He spoke with brotherly candor and without malice. "Sis hasn't anything to contribute anyway, except that she tackled the job of learning to walk like a soldier and is just about perfect now. Anyway, I think we'd rather listen to Mr. Amory. After all, he's really lived—made something of his life."

"No more than Dr. MacDonald," Mr. Amory retorted, ~eing the girl and deciding that she somehow resented young doctor's presence there. "Or, for that matter,

Kathy here. Or even Butch, who is still taking the hurdles as they come. We all have problems—some easy, some hard, some pleasant, some ugly, but all to be taken in stride. That's life. Here I am exhorting again. A habit, I suppose. Bear with me. I've been out of circulation for so long that I am afraid I'm not especially good company."

Dr. MacDonald left his chair and reached a hand to his mother. "I am sure of one thing," he said quietly. "We have stayed quite long enough, and it would be well to leave before Marshall, here, puts us out." He smiled at the nurse, and Kathy nodded in agreement, whereupon the others prepared to follow them from the room.

"I like your friends, Kathy," the patient told her, as the door closed behind them. "But I think I like Miss Barker best of all. Is she free, or is she, too, practically engaged to one of the doctors—Channing, perhaps?"

"What do you mean by 'she, too,' Mr. Amory?" Kathy asked, immediately on the defensive.

"Nothing, my dear," he answered quickly, "absolutely nothing. Is it a guilty conscience you have, or are you trying to evade the evidence? Don't answer that, Kathy. I have no right to tease you. I'm tired and hungry. Is there a possibility of food arriving soon?"

"It's late for dinner," Kathy told him. "I imagine the Resident advised the kitchen to delay your dinner for a while. I'll see about it at once."

She left the room and met the elevator coming up with the tray for 411A, so she returned with it to her patient and sat with him while he disposed of the food upon it.

"In another hour my relief will arrive," she told him, as he set his empty cup on the tray. "Don't stay up too long tonight, Mr. Amory. You have had a decidedly strenuous day. Sleep well. I'll carry this tray over to the dumb-waiter and be right back."

And then one day a glamorous woman was ushered into the room and with a low cry of delight threw herself before the chair in which David Amory sat. Kathy, who had been arranging the flowers about the room, turned in amazement. The newcomer had her arms about the patient and with her head on his chest was laughing and crying by turns.

"Marge. Marge, stop it!" the man cried, and Kathy

113

thought he sounded not only embarrassed but angry as well. "Don't tell me you have missed me that much!"

"Oh, I did, I did, David!" she cried. "I nearly died when they wouldn't let me come to you, wouldn't even tell me where you were. The beast—that man who claims to be your confidential secretary—told me you were seeing no one, not even me. Why, darling?" she demanded. "Tell me why you shut me out."

At last the man removed the clinging arms of his visitor and said amusedly, "We are no longer on the set, Marge. Calm yourself. I want you to meet my nurse, Miss Marshall, who, with certain members of the staff, is responsible for bringing me back from the dead. Mrs.— or is it 'Miss' again?" he asked. "Anyway, it is Marge Nichols—or was once."

The woman rose to her feet, turned to give the nurse an indifferent look, but said negligently, "Mr. Amory's friends owe you a debt of gratitude, Miss—er—Marshall." Then, turning back to Kathy's patient, she demanded, "When are you coming back, darling? I am here to see that you 'return at once. California air will be good for you. We need you. The place hasn't been the same since you left."

The man laughed. "Don't tell me I am still remembered out there, Marge," he said. "Ten years is a long time to be away from one's job and still be remembered. I don't believe you. And by the way, are you still working?"

A shadow seemed to fall over the glowing face of the visitor, and Kathy saw that she was no longer young. Now she shook her head. "I am resting right now, David, and really I have not seen a single part I would even for a moment consider. Anyway, I can afford to wait."

"And how is Gregory?" the man asked, somewhat warily.

The woman made a gesture intending to describe her complete detachment from Gregory. "All water over the dam," she murmured, "ages ago. I have completely forgotten him, poor boy!"

"And is there no one else? Have you not replaced him?"

"There is no one but you, darling," she replied. "There never was anyone but you, only I was———."

David Amory showed his amusement for a second time. Kathy wanted to creep out, but he motioned her to remain.

114

"Now Marge," he chided, "this is neither the time nor the place in which to display your acting ability. I have been a pretty sick man. I still am far from strong, and I can see my nurse feels that so much emotional display is not particularly good for me."

"You look perfectly well, David Amory," the visitor told him, glaring at his nurse. "And I am here to take you back. I saw your housekeeper and told her to get everything in order for your return within ten days. I told your secretary that I was coming to bring you back, and he had the effrontery to tell me to mind my own business. I want you to discharge him immediately. The idea! I am going to see about your immediate release from this place. We can take a leisurely trip across the country. Pedro is a careful driver and the car most comfortable. I chose it myself."

"Don't tell me that you drove to Bostwick from California, Marge! Not you!" the man explained.

"Of course not. I came by plane. I was impatient. Pedro is bringing the car east, and we can take our time on the way back, stopping when necessary or if you should become tired. But in a week or ten days now the country should be beautiful. It is lovely already on the West Coast."

Kathy spoke. "I doubt if Mr. Amory will be discharged right away, Mrs.—Miss Nichols. I understand it will be several weeks until he is considered well enough to leave."

"Who is your doctor—your Chief of Staff—the man who treated you, David?" the visitor demanded, sharply ignoring the nurse's comment. "I shall take the matter up with him, and we'll see what he has to say about it. I have some rights, and I intend enforcing them."

"Oh!" Kathy breathed, and wondered what her rights might be.

David Amory promptly enlightened her. His voice was sad and his face fell into haggard lines as he said quietly, almost grimly, "Miss Nichols was once, for a very brief time, my wife, or at least she was Mrs. David Amory. Her rights, as she calls them, are solely in her imagination, Nurse. I am tired. I wish to be alone."

Suddenly Kathy felt a wave of sympathy for the woman who had counted so much on this reunion and seen it fail. But her first duty was to her patient.

She said quietly, "You may come back later, Miss

115

Nichols," and opened the door for her departure. "Mr. Amory has been a very sick man, and while he is much better we must not allow him to take chances."

The woman hesitated for a moment, then walked swiftly to the open door, where she asked grimly, "Where can I find his doctor, Nurse?"

"I don't know exactly," Kathy answered, "but you may ask at the desk downstairs and have him paged."

Without another word the woman hurried down the long corridor to the elevator and disappeared. Kathy went back to arranging the flowers that had arrived in such abundance since her patient's convalescence had become known. A long sigh came from the man in the chair by the window.

"Marge *would* be the first to appear," he said bleakly, after a moment.

"She is very beautiful," the nurse said simply.

"And extremely selfish and entirely heartless."

Kathy said nothing. Apparently love had many guises, some of them far from beautiful. Or was it love this woman bore David Amory? She didn't know.

"I was new in the business, and she had suffered an unhappy love affair," the man said after a moment. "Our life together was wretched and ended quickly. She has since been successful in pictures, but her successive marriages have all ended disastrously. Do you know, Kathy, I don't even like her. I wish she would go back where she belongs. I have nothing to give her, not even friendship. Is that an unchivalrous statement to make? It is the truth. I wish I need never see her again. She spoiled for me the dream of married happiness. Probably she has spoiled it for other men as well. Is there anything you can do to make her leave me alone, Kathy?"

The nurse stared at him in amazement and some consternation. "Why, I can put a NO VISITORS sign on your door, if you like, and have the Resident leave word at the desk you are seeing no one." At his nod, she put out the sign, and then added, "But this is merely postponing the day of decision, isn't it?"

"What decision am I supposed to make?" he asked.

Kathy smiled at him. "Your decision to return with her."

"I have made that already," he said grimly.

"Why, Mr. Amory!" his nurse teased, hoping to ease the tenseness and lift the feeling of tragedy permeating the room. "What has become of your boasted ability to manage females, to achieve your own ends and get your own way? Don't tell me you are slipping!"

The man laughed without mirth, then said tersely, "You don't know Marge."

"Nonsense!" Kathy answered robustly. "No one can make you do anything you don't want to. Even our Chief of Staff couldn't make you release me for other duties. What are you scared of? She can't kidnap you, not from this hospital."

A long sigh was his answer. Whether it was one of relief or of despair she couldn't tell, for there came a peremptory knock on the door, and when Kathy went to open it Marge Nichols stood outside, an angry light in her eyes.

"And what is the idea of that sign?" she demanded, pointing disdainfully at the one Kathy had placed before the door.

"It means just what it says, Miss Nichols," the nurse told her calmly. "My patient is exhausted. He needs rest."

"I can't find his doctor," the irate visitor went on. "I don't like this place, and I shall tell David as much." She made a move to enter, but Kathy barred the way.

"I hope my patient is sleeping," she said, almost regretfully. "He needs plenty of rest and sleep and complete freedom from excitement and disquieting episodes. Oh, here comes Dr. Channing now." She motioned to the Resident to come forward quickly. "This is Dr. Channing, Miss Nichols," she introduced. "I am sure he will bear me out in insisting that our patient is still unfit to leave the hospital and should be kept free from disturbances of every sort."

"Do you have to put words into his mouth?" the woman demanded truculently. "I am quite able to take care of this, Nurse," she went on, " and if your patient is in such a grave condition perhaps it would be wise if you returned to him. Dr. Channing, I want to talk to you. Is there some place where we can discuss my husband's condition without interruption?"

"But he isn't your husband," Kathy exclaimed indignantly, and saw the astonishment in the Resident's face.

"That's what you think," the visitor snapped. "I have always considered him my husband and still do." She turned and walked down the corridor, while the Resident gazed at the nurse, a puzzled frown on his face.

"She's a rather terrible person, Doctor," Kathy murmured softly. "She was once his wife for a short time, years ago—she has had several husbands since, but he's afraid of her now. Keep her away from him, if you can. She's a dangerous woman. Better beware," she added.

David Amory sat with his head back and his eyes closed, and Kathy hoped he was indeed asleep. Without moving or opening his eyes, he asked wearily, "Has she gone, Kathy?"

"Dr. Channing is taking care of her, Mr. Amory," she told him. "You have nothing to fear. Your doctor and nurse will guard you." She said it whimsically, and the patient stared at her almost resentfully.

"You think I'm a moral coward, don't you?" he demanded.

"I think you are still far from well," was his nurse's reply.

"All right, all right, only don't leave me."

"I won't—not right away, at least," the girl told him. And with that he had to be content.

It was later that same afternoon that a tall, middle-aged black-haired man came to room 411A accompanied by the Resident and asked admittance. Kathy stood guard and opened the door a mere crack.

"Hello, there Dave!" the stranger cried, looking into the room over the nurse's head. "How are they using you? Want to see me, or shall I go roll my hoop some more?"

"Jim! Oh, Jim!" the patient cried jubilantly. "Come on in! You're a sight for weary eyes, boy. I have been hoping you would come."

"Then why in time didn't you send for me?" the man demanded, placing his free hand on their clasped ones. "After all, you're my boss, Dave. You pay my very generous salary each month. I've been plenty worried about you, but it wasn't until your ex-wife stormed into my office that I felt you needed me, so I hopped a plane and here I am—and not a moment too soon, from what Doc tells me. Don't let her get you down, Dave. Leave everything to me. I'll handle her!"

"Oh, Jim—James R. Fielding—this is my doctor and my nurse, two of the world's best. I owe my life to them, to their care and patient understanding. Dr. Channing is the Resident here, and Kathy Marshall is my favorite nurse and confidante as well. Don't go far, Kathy," he called after them, as the door closed. "I may need you."

"I guess we've spoiled him between us," the Resident said, as they left the room. "but he's such a swell guy, so likeable and appreciative of everything done for him. I was surprised to hear the Chief say much the same thing, Marshall. Only Dr. Blaine thinks his being here has added to the prestige of Memorial. After all, the hospital is his great love, I suppose. It comes first in his life."

"I suppose it does." Kathy agreed. "But it was a surprise to me that I was allowed to remain on this case for so long."

"That's the reason, Marshall," the Resident said. "It's Amory's reputation. And now that the world knows of his recovery, more honor and glory will be added to Memorial and of course indirectly—though not so indirectly, either —to the Chief of Staff. Dr. Blaine's a canny soul, Marshall, who grabs everything in the way of glory that may be floating around loose." He laughed at his own wit and went on to the elevator, while Kathy sat down with the floor nurse at the desk in the alcove.

CHAPTER FOURTEEN

"SO 'THE GREAT LOVER' has at long last departed," Irene Barker said, as she helped herself to an alluring chocolate from the huge box on Kathy's window sill. "Did he hate leaving, Kathy?" she asked, licking her fingers childishly. "You certainly spent enough time with him. Anyone else would have been promptly squelched for even suggesting it. Do you know, Kathy, I was disappointed in him. I had a sort of let-down feeling after I left his room that day. Time certainly has taken its toll in his case, all right."

"Do you think so?" Kathy asked, surprised. "Why, everyone else who saw him said he hadn't changed a bit, that the years had been extremely kind to him."

"Liars, every one of them," the older nurse murmured,

119

already choosing another sweet from the box. "But I will say he has good taste when it comes to candy. Aren't you eating any?"

Kathy shook her head. "Not just now, but go right ahead. I have a notion he expected me to share it with the others. I'm sorry, though, that you were disappointed in him. I thought he was wonderful. I shall never forget him. . . . Do you know, Irene?" she went on. "That is the only thing I dislike about this job. You become attached to a patient and suddenly he ups and leaves you cold. There's no such thing as a lasting friendship established between nurse and patient, I suppose. Or, for that matter, between doctor and patient, although that isn't exactly the same, is it?"

"I'll say not, from what I hear of MacDonald and the Adams gal," Irene said. "Mm! That was a good one. Pineapple, a huge chunk of it. Better have some before it gets stale or vanishes altogether." She searched for another of like ingredients and sighed when she discovered there were no more. "Have you talked with either party lately, Kathy?" she asked, her mouth full.

Kathy shook her head. "I've been far too busy, and now that the dance and bazaar is less than a week away I don't see much prospect of going over there. What have you heard that I haven't?"

"Not much. It seems one of the girls met the doctor and the ex-invalid at the Country Club a couple of weeks ago, and they certainly appeared to be infatuated with each other's company. I'll tell you something else. I'm mighty glad it isn't you Gary MacDonald is interested in. The grapevine has it that the Chief is doing his best to fox every operation MacDonald does here. Did I tell you about MacDonald's taking a patient of his away from Memorial and entering her in Saint Luke's? I guess that was the payoff. They tell me the Chief was fit to be tied and ordered MacDonald brought before the Board for discipline or what-have-you."

"But why should Dr. MacDonald do such a thing, Irene?" Kathy wanted to know. "Surely Memorial is much better equipped for operations than Saint Luke's, although I know the latter is a fine hospital. Who was the patient, and what was the operation for? I haven't heard anything lately. Tell me."

"Well, the woman was from the country, somewhere off the beaten track, and her sister here in Bostwick wanted her to see MacDonald about a growth of some sort. So Mac made an appointment for her to come here and submit to X rays, observation, et cetera, and then he decided an immediate operation was indicated. Well, it seems the Chief had other ideas. I don't know all of them, but one was to the effect that MacDonald wasn't qualified either to diagnose correctly or operate efficiently. An argument arose, and neither would give in, and so our boy wonder up and whisks his patient off to Saint Luke's and there he operated —successfully, too, and the patient is convalescing nicely, thank you. . . . If you don't hide this candy I'll burst, Kathy Marshall," she cried. "Here, before you move it out of temptation, give me just one more. Thanks!"

"And Dr. MacDonald? How about him? Is he still around? I haven't seen him lately."

"And won't if the Chief has his way," Irene said. "He informed MacDonald that he had acted in a high-handed manner and it would be better if he took all of his future cases to Saint Luke's. From what I gathered, MacDonald didn't answer him. Simply walked out. So much for that. The Chief wins again, darn him!"

"I'm sorry for both of them," Kathy murmured, shutting the drawer on the candy box.

"You haven't heard the last of it yet, my friend," the older nurse told her. "Wait until the story leaks out to the general public. Wait until Gary's aunt's husband—*the* Sam Bostwick—hears about it. I bet there will be fireworks aplenty then. So don't worry about your friend MacDonald yet awhile."

"I'm not worrying. What I know of Dr. MacDonald makes me very sure that he isn't going to run crying to his uncle over this, Irene," she said slowly. "He strikes me as a young man who will insist on killing his own snakes, as the saying goes."

"Maybe so, maybe so," Barker answered, and groaned aloud as there came a peremptory knock on the door. "We're busy, you, whoever you are," she cried. "Stay out!"

The head of a grinning student nurse came through the door opening, with the announcement that they were both wanted in the Superintendent's office at once. The head

121

was withdrawn, and the two nurses stared at each other questioningly. Now what?

Neither was particularly worried. It was probably the bazaar and more plans to be carried out. They felt they would be glad when the affair was over and they could settle down to their own concerns. But the spring bazaar and dance netted the staff considerable money, and they knew it was a necessary evil.

As it turned out, Miss Merriman had received fresh lists of volunteers—additions to the Bostwick doctors' wives who always served in an advisory capacity and, much to the chagrin of the real workers, received far more credit than was their due; but of course they had to be invited to participate. Then there were the members of the Board, most of them old and somewhat crabbed but important to the welfare of the institution, and they had to be asked, as usual, to act as a reception committee.

"Of all the cut and dried arrangements!" Irene muttered, as they left the Superintendent's office later. "Just what are you and I supposed to do anyway? Help Mrs. Moffitt, the late psychiatrist's widow, and old Doc Winthrop's sister dispense tea and sandwiches. Why don't they give the job to some of the student nurses? Why pick on us?"

Kathy shook her head. "Oh, it won't hurt us, I suppose. At least we'll get around to see everyone who's there. What are you going to wear, Irene? I thought I'd christen my last birthday present. I haven't had a chance to wear it yet."

"Why don't they let us wear uniforms? At least they'll wash. I don't feel like investing any money in this affair," the older nurse said. "And if you'll take my advice, Kathy, you'll wear something you don't care too much about spoiling. I've had several dresses ruined at these bazaars. Somehow I'm always given the job of passing sloppy stuff, and as sure as shooting someone either bumps into me or manages to knock my tray so that I get most of what's liquid on the front of my frock. I have been keeping my fingers crossed, hoping that this year I wouldn't have to help serve. I thought maybe I could simply eat, drink, and be merry without its costing me anything. Such a life! But take my advice and don't christen your new frock at this brawl. You'll have plenty of chances to display it, never fear."

122

"I wonder why uniforms are out, Irene?" Kathy murmured. "After all, it's a hospital affair and we're nurses. Such queer ideas some people have! Maybe you're right. I should hate having my new frock spoiled. Mother chose it for me and she has excellent taste. I have a notion it cost plenty, too."

"Lucky you!" the other muttered, as they parted outside Kathy's door.

And Kathy Marshall knew that she was indeed lucky in being a member of such a wonderful family, in being young and attractive, and in having Irene Barker for a friend.

It was later, when she was changing into uniform before dinner that same night, that she recalled what Irene had told her of this fresh difficulty that had arisen between the Chief and Dr. MacDonald. Just why should there be such enmity? They were both exceptionally clever surgeons and should be able to work together without friction. She wondered about that old story of the Chief's infatuation for Gary's mother—how he hated Gary's father and later ousted him from Memorial. How had he been able to do it? Oh, well, it was none of her business, just as this new affair should not concern her. She shrugged it off and went down the stairs to wait for Irene.

The big gymnasium was bright with color. Booths along two sides of the huge room displayed many things. There was homemade candy, cakes, and rolls, presided over by the young Mrs. Jepson, wife of Saint Luke's anesthetist and bride of a year. She was pretty and vivacious, and a few of the Memorial bigwigs shook their heads disapprovingly, but it wasn't long until her booth was empty of everything except the bride, who smiled happily at everyone, feeling sure of her success. Sales of goods in some of the other booths moved more slowly, but the auxiliary rallied to the rescue and no doubt found themselves eventually with many knickknacks for which they had little or no use, but it was for the good of the cause and the booths were emptied long before time for the dance to begin.

Irene Barker's usually serene face wore a questioning frown as she searched for Kathy Marshall in the crush. The younger nurse had been carrying trays of tea and sandwiches for hours and had seemed tireless, but now, suddenly, she had disappeared.

Dr. Elliott touched her arm. "Where's Kathy?" he demanded. "Is she on duty? Didn't she come? I've looked everywhere for her."

"And when did you arrive, Doctor?" Irene asked, somewhat ironically. "Didn't she give you tea and sandwiches? She may be only one of a dozen waitresses, but I bet a dollar it was she who fed most of this mob."

"I just got here," the young man told her, his gaze scanning the room. "Someone had to run things upstairs, and I seem to have been elected. I wonder where she went to."

He walked away, still searching, and Irene picked up a freshly laden tray and wondered who would be the next one to give either her or the tray a shove and douse her afresh. She had come to hate these flossy affairs. Why couldn't people come here and buy the stuff on display without having tea thrust down their throats? Ah, there came the Adams girl and Dr. MacDonald! She wondered if the Chief was around and if he had seen him. Oh, well, let them fight it out between them. Her feet hurt!

Glory be! The tea dispensers were getting up from the tables. Tea was evidently over, and this was the last tray she would have to tote around the room. Already strange men were removing booths, tables, and chairs and carting them off to the service elevator.

She stood somewhat apart, the now-empty tray dangling from one hand. People milled about, getting in each other's way, but miraculously the big room was cleared, a sedate row of chairs stood along the walls, and a five-piece orchestra appeared and settled on a small dais at one end of the room and began a somewhat raucous tuning-up.

"You look fit to drop, Irene," Dr. Channing said, softly taking the tray from her lax fingers and dropping it behind a convenient palm. "Been working you to death, I have no doubt. Come on upstairs for a few minutes, and I'll get you something to eat. Marshall and Elliott have a small table in the diet kitchen. What happened to your dress, for heaven's sake?"

"The usual thing," the nurse told him. "It happens every year. So Dr. Elliott found Kathy? He was down here looking for her. And by the way, where did she go so suddenly, and for that matter where have you been all afternoon?"

"Oh, I've been busy," he answered. "What a mob! Do people expect to dance here?"

"Some of them will leave—go home or go someplace else. They always have. There will be plenty of space for dancing a little later. Let's go get that food. I'm starved and my feet hurt."

"Your feet? I have never heard you complain of them before," the Resident said. "Maybe we'd better not plan on doing much dancing then."

His tone showed his disappointment, and Irene said quickly, "Oh, just a moment's respite will make me good as new, Doctor—Bob." She added his name a bit shyly.

"O.K." His hand beneath her elbow assisted her up the stairs to the kitchen.

The room was empty except for Dr. Elliott and Kathy Marshall, who greeted the newcomers with enthusiasm and helped gather the necessary food and other ingredients.

"I feel like a new woman," Kathy said, as she drained her second cup of coffee. "Here, let me serve you two," she went on, pushing back her chair from the table and preparing to get up. But Dr. Elliott jumped to his feet and laid a restraining hand on her shoulder.

"Not you," he said firmly. "You've been serving all afternoon. I'll wait on our guests. What will you have? We helped ourselves to sliced chicken, probably reserved for the cook's late snack; plenty of good strong coffee with cream and sugar. I made this young lady have her coffee with all the trimmings this time. How about you, Barker? Same for you? I know Channing takes his well creamed and sweetened."

He was soon busy making thick sandwiches which he placed before them, and when the kettle boiled he poured coffee for them all. It was a joyous meal, and they gave no thought to possible future punishment. This was now, a happy now. Tomorrow could take care of itself. And then, as they were stacking the dishes on the table, the door opened and Dr. Blaine entered, his face a thundercloud.

"And may I ask the meaning of this?" he demanded, glaring from one to the other but appearing to concentrate on the Resident.

Dr. Elliott answered immediately, his voice clear and unequivocal. "The two nurses have been serving in the bazaar all afternoon, Chief, and had had nothing to eat. We took it upon ourselves, Dr. Channing and I, to see that the obvious neglect was remedied. Surely you don't object?"

"Certainly I object," the Chief said harshly. "But apparently the harm has already been done. I have this to say, however. Discipline in this hospital appears to have reached a low ebb, and steps will be taken immediately to lift it to its former level."

He turned to leave the room, but Irene said demurely, "Won't you have a cup of hot coffee, Doctor? It is very good."

He turned to stare at her for a moment, then sat down near the table. It was Dr. Channing who gave him a clean cup and added the rounded spoonful of instant coffee. Dr. Elliott poured in the boiling water, and the two nurses made thick sandwiches from the remains of the chicken. It all seemed unreal to the quartet, and as soon as the Chief was served they slipped out, but it wasn't until they were well out of hearing that laughter overcame them, and if it was a bit hysterical who could blame them?

"You understand, please," Dr. Elliott said in the Chief's harsh voice, "that this by no means establishes a precedent. There must be no more of it. Discipline must and will be maintained!"

"Hear! Hear!" applauded the Resident. He slipped his arm about the older girl and maneuvered her through the maze of dancers and across the big room.

It suddenly became a lovely party, and when the last dance was over and the guests gradually melted away, Irene Barker turned to Kathy, a whimsical smile on her pretty face.

"See?" she said, pointing first to the front of her once immaculate frock and then to that of her friend. "What did I tell you? If we had worn those new creations we would have ruined them, and we couldn't have had any better time than we had in these messy clothes. I feel sort of besotted, but I have discovered that the way to a man's heart is indeed through his stomach, as witness our revered Chief." She laughed reminiscently, and Kathy joined her. They were both tired and mounted the stairs to their rooms in the annex slowly.

"Gosh, but my feet hurt!" were the last words Kathy heard her friend say as they parted before her door. Inside her room Kathy promptly kicked off her own slippers. Her feet hurt, too. But wasn't it worth it? And as she knelt to pray before getting into bed, she knew a feeling of pity for her Chief, that strange lonely man who didn't know how to be friends with his fellow workers.

"Help me to be considerate of others, dear God," she prayed, "and give me strength and courage to meet each day with cheerfulness."

She slipped into bed and knew nothing more until the first summons to breakfast roused her. She stretched and lay for a moment trying to arrange her thoughts which, this early in the morning, were quite apt to be confused. But she didn't go on duty until night, so there was no reason for her getting up early. With a deep sigh of thankfulness, she turned over on her side and went back to sleep.

CHAPTER FIFTEEN

"Oh, Kathy, Kathy!" Dana Adams whispered ecstatically into her office telephone early one afternoon a few weeks after the hospital bazaar. "I have something wonderful to tell you. You first of all my friends, Kathy. Can anyone there hear me? It is still very secret and very new."

"I think I can guess, Dana," Kathy told her. "I have been expecting to hear it, and I feel sure you are both going to be wonderfully happy."

"He told you!" Dana wailed. "And he promised not to tell a soul except his mother. Wait until I see him again!"

"Listen, darling," Kathy said, "no one has told me anything. I think I didn't have to be told. I am happy for you both, Dana. It is wonderful and so right for you. May I tell Irene, my best friend here at Memorial?"

"And you may tell Dr. Elliott, too, if you like," Dana said mischievously. "Perhaps it will give him ideas. Can you come over tonight, Kathy?"

"No, I can't, Dana," Kathy replied. "You see, I go on duty at three this afternoon in Men's Surgical. But I'll call you again. Good-by, and all my best to you both."

Irene Barker came down the stairs as Kathy replaced the telephone in its cradle. "What's up?" she asked. "You look sort of—well, funny."

"I don't know why I should," the other said quickly. "I have just heard some extremely happy news."

"Then for heaven's sake tell me. I can stand a bit of happy news."

"Dana Adams and Gary MacDonald are engaged to be married. Dana is in seventh heaven. I'm so happy for her, and for him, too."

"I can't say that you look particularly radiant," Irene retorted, examining Kathy's brooding expression. "Don't tell me you retain any romantic ideas about that guy, especially after knowing Bill Elliott. Now there's a man after my own heart—clever, amusing, and I bet he's kind to his mother. You're something of a dope, Kathy Marshall," she went on emphatically. "It was just because of that appealing boyish manner, so deceptive in a doctor. I'm glad the die is cast, and you can now erase him from your consciousness. Bill Elliott is worth two of him. Why, Dr. Channing thinks the world of Elliott. Says he's his own man and will go far in his profession. What are you laughing at?" she demanded, as the younger nurse giggled.

"At you," she replied, "trying to sell me a bill of goods. And listen, Irene Barker," she went on, a bit heatedly, "I am not now and never was the least bit romantically interested in Gary MacDonald. I liked him—I still like him. That's all, and if anyone's a dope it's you for imagining things."

A profound sigh was the only answer to the other's statement.

As they parted, Miss Merriman came to them, her face pale. "There has been an accident, a terrible accident!" she breathed. "The Chief—Dr. Blaine——"

The two nurses stared at each other, then turned and raced to the desk, where already a frightened group had gathered. The heavy front door opened and Dr. MacDonald entered, hurried to the elevator, and disappeared at once. Dr. Elliott called to Irene Barker, and they, too, disappeared. Kathy felt deserted and somewhat forlorn. Why wasn't she in on this? But she knew that there wasn't a better nurse in an emergency than Irene Barker, and apparently this was an emergency. She tried to hear what the others were saying. Something about a collision, a car turning over in the ditch, someone being killed, and someone else badly injured? Which was which? She didn't hear, and no one appeared to notice her.

The telephone shrilled and someone said, "Yes, Doctor. I'll have her paged at once." The girl turned, scanned the group around the desk, and asked, "Is Marshall here? Oh," she said, when Kathy lifted a hand, "you're wanted in 411A immediately."

Kathy flew to the elevator and pressed the button marked four. She had no idea who might be in 411A. She knew only that she was needed.

The elevator stopped and she stepped out to confront the Superintendent of Nurses.

"Dr. Blaine has been badly hurt, Marshall," the white-faced woman said. "X rays show multiple injuries. He is in the main O.R., and we expect to move him into 411A. Please see that the room is in readiness. You are to have the first eight-hour period, from three to eleven, with Moore, who, we feel, is our most experienced nurse."

Kathy knew that 411A was ready for any new occupant, but she dutifully followed Miss Merriman's instructions to see that everything was in order.

It was later that the door opened and the Superintendent came into the room.

"Just how badly is he injured, Miss Merriman?" Kathy asked tentatively. One didn't ask questions at Memorial; one did what one was told to do. But this was the Chief, and Kathy felt that she must know.

"It is not entirely clear at this time," Miss Merriman replied. "His back, we fear; several ribs broken; perhaps the right hip fractured; and, what is the worst of all, certainly the most tragic, his right hand and arm—his wonderful operating hand—mangled." Her voice shook with emotion.

Kathy gasped, "Oh, no! Not that!"

There were sounds of movement in the corridor outside, and Miss Merriman held the door open while the stretcher was wheeled in and the Chief placed in the bed. Kathy fought a rising sob. He looked so big, so white, and so helpless, this man who had brought life and health to so many. Barbara Moore, one of the older nurses, stood by the bed, her eyes on the patient's face. Dr. MacDonald was beside her, his hand on the Chief's pulse.

"I think he will sleep through the rest of the afternoon and evening, Moore," he murmured, replacing the hand. "If you need me, I shall be right here. He is not to be left alone. You understand? Watch closely for any change." Moore nodded, and he turned to smile gravely at Kathy before he left the room.

Kathy wondered just why she should have been assigned to this case. Moore was capable and quite able to handle it. But evidently the Chief rated two specials, during the first trick at least.

The hours dragged. The Resident came in at seven, and Dr. MacDonald returned soon after. The nurses took turns in eating their supper and remained on close watch until the relief arrived.

Kathy was surprised to see Irene Barker enter the room. A student nurse followed her.

Moore muttered, "Here's hoping the Chief doesn't wake up until you're off duty, Barker." She grinned and motioned to the student.

"He should be thankful to get anyone," Irene told her. "Six specials indeed! It's ridiculous. But that's Annie's orders, and there wasn't another R.N. available." She shrugged and picked up the patient's chart. "H'mm," she murmured. "Run along, you two. We'll manage all right." She, too, smiled briefly at Kathy and sat down beside the sleeping patient.

The student nurse opened her textbook and tried to study but gave it up. The Chief was groaning. The Resident came in soon after one A.M. and reported everything going as well as could be expected, but still the patient continued to moan. The student nurse looked scared and when Dr. MacDonald arrived a little later, he suggested a shot of morphine. After that the patient became quiet, and there was little or no disturbance for the remainder of the night.

At six in the morning Miss Merriman appeared. She had evidently slept badly and looked pale and worn in the morning sunshine. She examined the patient's chart, found it heartening, and asked softly what Dr. MacDonald thought about the Chief's hand. Irene told her that nothing had been decided, and after a moment the Superintendent left the room.

It was a few minutes after seven that the day nurse arrived. She was alone. Irene grinned tiredly at her and motioned that there were two of them during the previous watches.

"They ran out of doubles," Reed told her cynically. "All nonsense, anyway. Why should he, just because he happens to be Chief, get every available nurse to serve him? I can manage the old duffer, and don't you make any mistake about it. He isn't going to die," she went on. "He's far too cussed to give up his job here at Memorial. Although I guess his days of surgery are over, aren't they?"

Irene put a finger to her lips. "The opiate is wearing off, Reed," she said softly. "MacDonald should be in any minute now. That guy never seems to sleep." She turned to the student nurse. "Come on, Peterson, let's go get some breakfast. Good luck!"

They left the room and met Dr. MacDonald in the corridor. He stopped for a minute, and Irene reported all she knew about the patient. When she had completed her account of the night's happenings, she asked, "Do you think he will live, Doctor? Do you think he is going to recover and be all right?"

The young man shook his head. "I believe he will recover," he told her gravely, "but I doubt if he will be the same. After all, he is no longer young but in his sixties, I understand, and people of that age haven't the recuperative powers they once had. But we intend doing our best, Barker, and if he isn't satisfied we can call in surgeons from outside. Run along and get to bed," he urged. "You look about ready to drop."

"I am tired," Irene confessed, "and I'm hungry, too." She decided it wasn't the time to congratulate him on his engagement, and let it ride.

The student nurse had vanished, but Irene saw her later in the almost deserted dining room, where she was consuming quantities of hot buttered toast and scrambled eggs. Irene grinned at her. What it was to be as young as that and able to eat such a breakfast! She sat down opposite, and the main brought her fruit juice and inquired as to what she wanted.

"Oh, bring me a slice of toast—skimp the butter, Agnes—and a cup of clear coffee, strong. Don't bring either cream or sugar."

"Diet again?" the maid asked, shaking her head disapprovingly. "Don't. . . . No man's worth it, Miss Barker," she added, as she hurried away.

"Sa-ay!" Irene cried, but the kitchen door was already shut. "The nerve of that one!" she muttered. "And yet why else am I doing it? By jinks, I'm hungry. I'll have the works. Butter, cream, and sugar and maybe a molasses cookie. That'll show her!"

Agnes came back with the toast—two slices of it, both well buttered—a pot of coffee, and sugar and cream as well. "Here you are, Miss Barker," she said, as she set the tray down on the table. "Mrs. Bunting is just taking some swell ginger cookies out of the oven, and I'll bring you a couple." Her face was devoid of expression, and Irene Barker wondered if she had dreamed that remark about a man.

"Thank you, Agnes," she said, and poured her coffee gratefully. It smelled good and was strong as she liked it.

"Funny hours you nurses have here," Agnes said, after a moment. "Not that it makes any difference, I suppose. There's food around here all the time. How bad was the big boss damaged, Miss Barker?" she asked.

"It was a bad accident," the nurse told her noncommittally. "Who was the other casualty, do you know? I believe he was killed instantly."

Agnes shook her head. "No one around here. I heard he was driving one of those trailer trucks—you know, the kind that sways from side to side and wants the whole earth. I guess the boss' swell new car was smashed completely. Too bad, but he could afford it better than most of us lesser guys. I hope he gets over it all right—not that I even know him," she went on, "but they say—yes, Mrs. Bnting, I'm coming. Darn her!" she muttered, as she moved not too rapidly toward the kitchen, "She's a regular slave driver."

"You don't mean that, Agnes," Irene murmured, but if the maid heard she gave no sign. And yet, the nurse asked herself tiredly, aren't we all slaves to one thing or another —duty, friends, family and—and love?

She finished her breakfast and went up to her room in the annex. As she passed Kathy Marshall's door, she listened for a moment, then turned the door handle and looked in. The younger nurse, in robe and slippers, was sitting before the window, eyes dreamy and lovely face pensive.

Irene entered softly. "Am I intruding, Kathy?" she asked.

Kathy turned with a start, then stretched slim arms high above her bright head. "You never intrude, Irene," she replied affectionately. "Was it pretty bad last night? You look done in. Take a warm bath and hop into bed."

"I intend doing just that," the other said, "but I just wanted to do a bit of comparing. Have you heard how serious the damage is?"

Kathy shook her head. "Miss Merriman mentioned broken ribs, injured back, a possible fracture of the right hip, and—what worried her most—the mangling of his right hand and arm. Is that about right, Irene? What a tragedy if he loses the use of his hand!"

"MacDonald says he is going to save that hand if it is humanly possible," Irene said. "By the way, his back is merely strained—painful but not too serious—and the hip isn't broken. But he is pretty badly bruised and lacerated, and then the shock has to be taken into account. He's no longer a young man. However, I'm wondering if the Chief will even let Mac treat him at all. I don't know who sent for him in the first place. There are other surgeons available around here, and knowing the Chief's enmity for Mac I wonder anyone had the temerity to call him in. It would be just like Bill Elliott to do it. He considers the feud between those two unethical in the extreme, but just the same it sort of places his nibs in a tight spot. Not that I'm holding any briefs for the Chief, you understand——"

"It is all extremely silly, Irene," Kathy interrupted emphatically. "All that trouble occurred ages ago. I doubt if any surgeon could do more for our Chief than Dr. MacDonald. But do you really think there will be trouble?"

"It all depends," the other murmured slowly. "Let us hope and pray that there wont be—that somehow, some way, the old war horse will suffer a complete change of heart. Here's hoping, anyway. Night, Kathy. See you sometime. Are you still on that trick with Moore?"

"As far as I know," Kathy replied.

The door closed after the older nurse, and Kathy began to dress slowly. She was glad to know that Gary MacDonald was to treat the Chief. She somehow felt that if anyone could save that precious right hand, he could. But would Dr. Blaine carry his animosity so far as to refuse his assistance? And yet the older surgeon knew how efficient the younger man was. He had come to Memorial from a big metropolitan hospital bearing flattering credentials, refusing to allow any connection with his aunt's husband who was wintering in the south to sway the Board's decision. Yes, Kathy said to herelf, she was glad to know Dr. MacDonald was on the job, and she wondered if indeed that miracle-working hand could be saved for future service.

On her way out of the hospital a little later, she stopped at the Superintendent's office to discover that Barbara Moore had been assigned to another case but that Kathy was to take 411A.

"Alone?" she asked impulsively, and bit her lip.

"Alone," the Superintendent replied. "We are all very happy to know that conditions are not nearly as bad as we feared. The hip, while badly bruised is not fractured as suspected, the ribs have been firmly strapped, and everything that seems possible at this time done for the right arm and hand. You proved so efficient in the nursing of a former patient with a similar injury—Latham, I believe the name was — that we decided you and Dr. Elliott should be given charge of Dr. Blaine, at least for part of the time. I doubt if any more twelve-hour duty will be necessary." She smiled faintly. "You are a most satisfactory nurse, my dear, and we appreciate you. I hope you realize that."

"Th-thank you, Miss Merriman," Kathy stammered. She was far too astonished to say anything more.

She turned to leave the room and stopped, as the Superintendent went on, "No doubt you have heard a certain amount of gossip. Perhaps I should not mention it at this time, but I want you to understand how things are." The woman paused and seemed to fumble for words.

Kathy spoke impulsively. "You mean the supposed enmity between the Chief and Dr. MacDonald?"

The Superintendent nodded, then shook her head. "Refuse to recognize it," she said firmly. "There is no place for either enmity or dislike in a hospital, in the caring for the sick and injured, and certainly not between men of integrity such as we have here in Memorial. I trust you will hold this conversation in strictest confidence, Marshall. It is as if nothing pertaining to the personal lives of anyone had ever been mentioned. Thank you for stopping in."

Kathy Marshall left the Superintendent's office in

something of a daze. So she was to be alone with the Chief from three this afternoon until eleven at night. Why had she been chosen for that ordeal? Surely her care in the Bob Latham case was not recommendation enough, and yet what else? To be sure, she was a good nurse. She prided herself on that fact, but she acknowledged now that she was frightened at the prospect of nursing the stricken Chief. She had always been afraid of him, afraid of his sharp tongue and fiery glances.

She opened the front door and slipped out into the bright spring day. Perhaps a brisk walk would restore her assurance and give her courage, for she knew without the shadow of a doubt that she would need both during that long eight hours from three until eleven.

CHAPTER SIXTEEN

APPARENTLY THE PATIENT was sleeping when Kathy Marshall entered 411A that afternoon, and Myrtle Reed grinned wryly, crossing two of her fingers as a sign the Chief had not been in the best of humor. Kathy experienced a sudden wavering of her hard-won courage. She examined the chart and found that the patient had refused certain prescribed medications and taken but little liquid nourishment. She knew that last didn't mean much this early, even though the Chief had the reputation of being a good trencherman.

"God be with you!" Reed murmured, as she opened the door to leave. Dr. MacDonald barred her way. "Oh, oh!" she breathed, "I'm sorry" and she fled down the long corridor.

The young surgeon was smiling quizzically as he came into the room. "Not but what we all need Him, Marshall," he said softly, "but why was it necessary to remind you of the fact?"

"Oh, she meant nothing particularly personal, Doctor." Kathy replied, her voice low. "It is often used here in Memorial during difficult cases. We think of it more as a blessing than anything else."

"I see," the man murmured, scanning the chart and looking closely at the patient.

Kathy suddenly noticed that the eyelids of the Chief were not entirely closed. There was a slit of blue discernible. In spite of the bandages, his face looked grim, or perhaps it was just her imagination. He moved slightly and groaned aloud.

Dr. MacDonald asked quietly, "Is there anything I can do for you, Doctor?"

There was no response for a moment, and the young surgeon didn't move. At last the patient muttered almost unintelligibly, "My hand. Is it going to be all right?"

"We are going to do our best, Doctor."

"Don't quibble. Is it or is it not?" His voice was harsh and the half-open steely eyes defied anyone to try to deceive him. Kathy held her breath.

"It will never be as good as it was before," Dr. Mac-Donald told him evenly. "It will be usable, however. We can promise no more at the present time. The palm is severely torn and one bone in the wrist shattered, necessitating its removal, as well as the amputation of the small finger. The rest of the hand can be saved—will be saved."

"Then it is your opinion that I am done for?" the man demanded, still harshly, after a long moment.

"By no means," Dr. MacDonald replied emphatically. "Your brain is uninjured and is still of incalculable value to the hospital and to mankind."

"Teacher?" he jeered.

"Not entirely. Rather, advisor—surgeon emeritus."

The patient's eyes closed, and his mouth was grim. For a long moment there was a pregnant stillness in the hospital room. No one moved, and at last the Chief whispered raspingly. "Sure?"

"Yes, Doctor, I'm sure. Do you wish other medical advice? It is your privilege."

"Rot!" the man cried explosively. "Think I want a lot of those half-baked sawbones gloating over my downfall? "Who's looking after this hand of mine? Where's Elliott and Marshall? They did a good job on young Latham. Send Elliott in. Come in back in an hour, Doctor," he added, after a minute in which he seemed to be debating something in his own mind. "I want the whole story in detail. It's your turn to gloat but I can take it, Doctor, I can take it."

"Nonsense!" Gary MacDonald said crisply. "We're surgeons, both of us. Personal feelings have no place in our work. Understand? I'll get Dr. Elliott at once. He's a good man. I'm glad he is available."

The door closed behind him, and the patient groaned again. Kathy went to him. "Can I do anything, Doctor?" she asked softly. "Are you in pain?"

"Nothing you would understand, Marshall," he muttered, and Kathy saw that his eyes were tightly closed while his head moved from side to side in a motion of hopeless despair. The girl's heart ached for him, and she impulsively smoothed back the heavy gray hair from his forehead, her touch as gentle as a mother's. The head became quiet but the eyes remained closed, and a long sigh escaped him.

Kathy kept up the gentle massage, and at last the man whispered, "That feels better. I—I am glad you are here, Marshall, you and Elliott. Do your best for my hand. Do your best . . . your best . . ." and Kathy knew that he dozed.

It was after six when Dr. Elliott arrived, but still the patient slept, and Kathy drew the young doctor into the corridor and related all that she had heard earlier.

"He has faith in you doctor," she told him, "and in me. He spoke of the Latham case and how we worked to save Bob Latham's hand. We've got to do as much for the Chief, Doctor," she said insistently, "we've got to."

"Dr. MacDonald rushed me right over here as soon as I came in from Pediatrics, Kathy," the young man told her. "We have three new cases of polio over there, and I've been plenty busy. We've had to enlarge the isolation section, but still there isn't room. Was there a Board meeting this afternoon, do you know?" he asked.

Kathy shook her head. "Postponed until the Chief is out of danger."

"How does he get on with Mac?"

"Nicely from what I gathered. Dr. MacDonald explained just what had happened to his hand and what had been done. He didn't soften it a bit—in fact, I thought he was almost brutally frank—but evidently it was what the Chief wanted. He nearly exploded when Dr. MacDonald suggested other advice, so I have an idea the enmity between them has been greatly exaggerated."

"Don't fool yourself, Kathy," Dr. Elliott told her. "The Chief hates Mac like poison, and while I think Mac isn't exactly fond of the old war horse, he's first of all a sur-

137

geon—nothing else matters to him. Mac's a swell guy, Kathy. I wish I had his ability."

Kathy smiled. "Funny thing, but Dr. MacDonald spoke equally well of you and your ability. How you doctors stick together! . . . Maybe the patient is awake."

They entered the dimly lighted room to find the patient still sleeping quietly, but Dr. Elliott gently touched brow and cheek of the unconscious man and nodded his head approvingly.

"Let him sleep, Kathy," he advised. "I'll be around if he wants me. Sleep will do him more good than talking right now. Poor chap!" he murmured, his face brooding.

Tears stung Kathy's eyelids, and she blinked rapidly to prevent them from falling.

"I'm glad you're on with me," the young man said softly, taking her hand in his for a moment. "We make a pretty good team, don't we? Together, Kathy?" He pressed her fingers while the girl said nothing, but she smiled fleetingly and with that he was forced to be content.

The patient slept until well after ten, when he complained that he couldn't understand why no one gave him anything to eat. He had no temperature and he was hungry. The nurse asked what he wanted, and he informed her that he would like a thick sandwich—chicken or ham but chicken, if possible—and a cup of good strong coffee with plenty of cream and sugar, too. Was it possible to have such things at this hour of the night, or was that privilege reserved for a favored few? Kathy told him she would personally get whatever he wanted, and that she would send Dr. Elliott in to visit him while she was gone.

Dr. Elliott laughed, when she told him of her patient's demand, then shook his head. "He'll live!" he promised. "O.K., I'll keep him company while you're gone, and," he called after her as she hurried toward the elevator, "make it a double order. My lunch was pretty meagre. Have you eaten?"

"Not yet," she answered. "Perhaps I'll make it a triple order—if the Chief doesn't object, that is."

"He won't," the young man answered, opening the door of 411A.

The diet kitchen was a beehive of activity. The nurses

who had been on call duty milled about, preparing trays for the night staff and incidentally snatching bites of their own lunches in the process. Kathy saw that there was very little chicken left and mentioned the fact that she was getting a lunch for the Chief, who desired chicken sandwiches.

"Gosh" one of the nurses cried. "Here, take mine—nothing but white meat, and I don't give a hoot if Marsden in Men's Surgical gets chicken or ham. She's lucky to get anything. How many do you want, Marshall? Two be enough?"

"If that's all there is it will have to be enough," Kathy answered, placing the two sandwiches on her tray. "Dr. Elliott, who is with him, and I will have to take ham and like it."

"Aw, come on, kids," one of the nurses cried contritely. "Let's hand over our chicken. After all, she has a really tough assignment, and we can afford to be generous for once."

"No, no," Kathy protested emphatically. "As long as the Chief has his chicken that'll be all that matters. Oh, well, maybe he can eat three or even four," as another nurse slipped two of her sandwiches to the Chief's tray. "He says he's hungry. Thanks, girls," she said, placing three pots of coffee beside the plate of sandwiches and adding cream and sugar. "You're a swell bunch, and I love every one of you."

It was an unusual speech for the generally reserved Marshall, and the nurses showed their astonishment. But Kathy didn't notice and left the kitchen, with her laden tray, unaware of the remarks that followed her.

"I'm flabbergasted," one of the younger nurses said as she completed her tray.

"Oh, she probably didn't mean it, not actually," another said skeptically. "Why should she? She's the teacher's pet around here and doesn't have to bother with any of us lesser fry."

"Me-ow!" jibed one of the older nurses, spreading mustard generously on the ham sandwiches she was preparing. "Marshall's a swell girl and has earned her place in the sun, and don't you make any mistake about it. Twelve-hour duty! Ye gods! Who else would have submitted to that grind? Not me, for one."

"But you forget the case she was on, Blauvelt. David Amory! A movie star! Think of it." It was the first speaker who pointed that out.

"What of it?" Blauvelt snapped. "Did you ever see him?" As the other shook her head, she went on," "He's been out of pictures for ages. He was before your time anyway and completely out of your class."

"And just what do you mean by that, Kate Blauvelt?"

"Not a thing, not a thing," Blauvelt replied, picking up her tray and moving toward the door. "Forget it."

One by one the nurses, laden with the lunches, filed out of the room, and the elevator whined, stopped, and whined again.

Back in 411A the Chief was savoring the first solid food since his accident. Occasionally Kathy warned him to take it easy, expecting to be told each time to mind her own business, but the patient merely frowned and went on nibbling at his lunch. His bed had been raised to allow for easier eating, but suddenly he asked to be lowered and Kathy complied quickly. After all, he had eaten only a little—part of one sandwich and a cup of coffee. It was just as well, she knew, but she looked anxiously at Dr. Elliott, who nodded approval and went on eating his own lunch. The Chief promptly went to sleep. Kathy carried the tray into the corridor, and Dr. Elliott followed.

"If the Chief isn't going to eat those sandwiches, I will," the young man announced, reaching for two of the three remaining on the tray. "Why let them spoil? And you didn't eat much yourself. What's the matter? Didn't you like them?"

"I wasn't hungry," the girl replied, "and I was worried about the Chief. Do you think he should have eaten anything at all so soon? After all——"

"He's a doctor as well as a surgeon, Kathy," the young man assured her. "He should have sense enough to know when he has had enough. You notice he didn't actually eat much. Don't worry, Kathy. Dr. Blaine's condition is perfectly satisfactory. I'll shove that tray down the dumbwaiter. Run back to your patient, and if he wants me I'll be around."

So Kathy returned to 411A and busied herself with the onerous requirements of a nurse on duty. Barker would be coming on at eleven, she told herself. She examined the man sleeping so quietly and wondered if he really had suffered a change of heart and disposition, as Bill Elliott had hinted. She wondered, too, whether or not the Board would consider his demand for Gary MacDonald's dismissal from the staff of Memorial and felt sure that it wouldn't not with Sam Bostwick as president of that body. She had heard that the Bostwicks were back from the south, and so he would undoubtedly be present.

A long sigh came from the patient, and the nurse bent over him. But the man merely shifted his position a bare inch and slept again. She was glad to know that his back was only strained, not broken, and that the hip joint had not been shattered as had at first been feared. The worst damage had been to the right arm and hand, and in the case of the Chief of Staff that was real tragedy.

The bells on Saint Matthew's Church chimed, and the patient stirred and swore faintly.

'What is it, Doctor?" Kathy asked. "What can I do for you?"

"My hand," he muttered thickly and tried to move it, but it was tightly bound against his side.

"Does it pain?" the nurse asked.

"Pain?" he growled. "What do you think? I'm going to lose it. It will have to be amputated. I tell you, this will be his revenge."

"No one is going to amputate your hand, Doctor," Kathy told him firmly, wishing Dr. Elliott would come but fearing to leave the patient to call him. But, as if he sensed her need, the door opened and Dr. Elliott entered.

"Tell him he isn't going to lose his hand, Doctor," Kathy said, with what she hoped was conviction.

"Of course not, Chief," the younger man said. "What ever gave you that idea? There was never any question of amputation. The wound is clean, and we have the means at hand to prevent infection. You have been dreaming, Doctor. There's a much better chance of saving your hand than there ever was of Bob Latham's, and yet his hand is entirely healed and he is back on his job. Not using it, of course, but supervising, and making a mighty good thing of it, too."

"My job, my job!" the Chief whispered bitterly.

"Oh, don't let us cross bridges until we reach them,"

141

Dr. Elliott said crisply. "That is what you have drilled into us, and now we will return the advice. We—Marshall and I—intend to nurse that hand, and you know what a good job we did on Bob Latham."

"He says it pains," Kathy murmured. "Can you help him?"

"How badly does it pain you, Doctor?" the younger man asked gently.

"Not too much—not more than I can bear, if I know I'm not going to lose it. You promise, Doctor, you promise? Swear to me that you will save my hand!" It was almost a wail and from such a man as Doctor Blaine it was heartbreaking to his nurse.

"How can I?" the other asked, realizing the patient's low spirits. "I'm not God, Chief. I can only speak as a physician who has seen much worse injuries than yours and watched them heal completely. Man, you're half asleep. Tomorrow you will laugh at your fears. Of course your hand will be saved, and you are going to help save it. Here, drink this," he advised, holding a glass to his lips. "It will quiet you, and you will sleep again. Don't shake your head at me, Dr. Blaine," he said in mock severity. "You are merely getting a dose of your own medicine. Take it like a man. Your hand is as right as we can make it at this time. In a month, or maybe less, the wound should be healed."

He winked at the anxious nurse opposite and nodded in the direction of the patient, who already was asleep.

CHAPTER SEVENTEEN

DR. BLAINE'S CONVALESCENCE was satisfactory, although rather hectic at times. No, Kathy Marshall told herself, his disposition had not changed very materially. He still glared at his nurses and doctors, and refused food and medications when the spirit moved him. But she found that she no longer feared him. In fact she found herself smiling at him during some of his sudden rages, and it wasn't long until he began to return her smile, if somewhat shamefacedly. In two weeks he was able to walk about the room, and he fumed at being confined.

Then, one unseasonably cool June day, the Board decided there must be a meeting to consider the Chief of Staff's successor, as well as to transact other business of importance. Did Dr. Channing think Dr. Blaine able to receive the Board? The Resident consulted the Chief and was told to bring them on. Dr. Blaine spoke even more harshly than customary, and Dr. Channing pitied him.

Over in the annex, late that morning, the telephone was ringing. When the maid managed to get to it, an excited voice remanded, "Is Kathy—Miss Marshall—there?"

"I don't know. I'll have to look. Who shall I say is calling?"

"Tell her it's Dana Adams, and please hurry. It's very important."

The maid ran up the three flights of stairs and, panting from the exertion, halted at Kathy Marshall's door. She rapped softly, then hearing nothing, turned the handle and found it unlocked. She opened it a crack and looked in. Kathy turned on her side and stared sleepily.

"Wh-what is it?" she asked.

"Telephone," the girl said succinctly. "Dana Adams wants you, and she said it was important. Shall I have her hold the line, or call later?"

Kathy swung her feet out of bed and into slippers and reached for a robe. "I'll come downstairs right now," she said. "Thanks for waking me. I was dead tired." She followed the maid to the telephone and listened while the ecstatic Dana talked.

"Gram is giving me an announcement party tomorrow night, Kathy. It's rather short notice, I know but she just decided and you have got to come. If it isn't your free night, change with someone else, because I simply will not have it without you. We are having the men, too. I knew Gary would want to be here, and so we are inviting some of our friends to help us celebrate. Pete's going to try to make it, but he wasn't sure he could. And, Kathy, darling, try to be kind to that brother of mine. We all know he's crazy about you, and after all he's only a couple of years younger than you are. Gram adores you, and I love you as much as I could ever love a sister. Oh, I know Dr. Elliott is mad about you but—well, Pete's a peach. Be sure to come early, won't you? I have so much to tell you—I want to tell you everything!"

"Thank you, Dana," Kathy replied. One sentence in the excited conversation rang in her ears. "Oh, I know Dr. Elliott is mad about you." Was he? Just where did

143

that leave her? And had she ever been even remotely interested—romantically—in Gary MacDonald? What sort
of a girl was she, anyway? She liked Bill Elliott, she was
sure of that, but weren't liking and loving vastly different?

All this flashed through her mind in a moment, until
Dana asked somewhat impatiently if she was still there
and why didn't she answer—she could come, couldn't
she?

Kathy said yes, it was her free night, and she would see
her later. She couldn't talk any longer now, because the
hall was cold and she was not dressed.

But as she went back to her room, she thought of
Dana's statements. Pete thought he was in love with her,
and Gram adored her, and Dana loved her as she would a
sister, and Bill Elliott was mad about her. She wondered
whimsically 'what Gary MacDonald's feelings were. Did
he, too, love her as he would a sister?

She got into bed for a few more minutes of sleep, but
no sleep came, and after an hour she got up, slipped into
the bathroom for a shower, then dressed and went downstairs in search of food. Irene Barker joined her, and the
two went in to lunch together.

"What's on for this afternoon, Kathy?" Irene asked,
as they found their seats at the table. "I feel like spending some money. Will you help me pick out a suit and
maybe a dress and a hat? I'm just about destitute and
never realized it until I began looking over my clothes
yesterday. Can do?"

Kathy hesitated for a moment, then nodded her head.
"I'd love it, Irene," she said. "Maybe I'll get a hat
myself. I'm sick of everything I have, and Mrs. Hammond is giving an announcement party for Dana and
Gary MacDonald—tomorrow night, no less. Imagine!
And I didn't get my invitation until an hour or two ago.
A sort of spur-of-the-moment affair, apparently. Whether
it's a dress occasion or not, I wouldn't know. But it isn't
a hen party, Irene. Some of Gary's friends are invited."

"Then for heaven's sake get a new dress, Kathy," her
friend advised. "There's nothing like a new frock to
perk up the old morale. Let's go to Madame Berthe's
first and see what she has." She ate sparingly of the
hearty lunch offered, saying as she so often did that she

must watch her figure, and the two nurses left the table before anyone else.

"What makes you think I need my morale perked up, Irene?" Kathy wanted to know. "Are you still laboring under the mistaken idea that I might be nursing a broken heart or a badly bruised one? I certainly don't understand why you ever got the idea in the first place, and I'm sure my past relationship with Dr. MacDonald, casual as it was, couldn't have given you any such impression. Do you know, Irene, it sort of puzzles me. Do I appear to need a morale builder?"

"Frankly, I don't know," the older nurse answered. "But let it pass. I can only warn you that if you still love the guy, don't attend any announcement party. Work, have pressing duty or an emergency, but don't put yourself through the agony of watching him make love to another girl. I wish I felt sure you were all over him—if there was anything to it in the first place. And I wish you would wake up to the fact that Bill Elliott's devoted to you. Bill's a grand guy, worth two of MacDonald. But I'm only an onlooker—an affectionate one, to be sure, but still an outsider, looking on."

"I wonder how the Board Meeting is going," Kathy said, as they passed two of the members near the entrance of the huge building.

"O.K." Irene shrugged. "Skip it. Anyway, I'll still pray for you, Kathy," she said whimsically. "And I do mean pray, for I'm sure you need it. And don't worry about the Board Meeting. If Sam Bostwick's on deck, everything will run smooth as greased lightning. That guy gets things done with the least amount of friction possible. I understand there is talk of building an addition to Pediatrics—an isolation ward for polio cases and such. We sure have needed it for a long time. Maybe it will be brought up at the Board Meeting. I wish I could be there—invisible, you know. I should like to hear who will be suggested for the Chief's job. There is a persistent rumor that Dr. Scott in Boston—that mysterious visitor who dropped in on us during the Latham hospitalization—is the favored candidate for the post. They say he's a whiz. Anyway, it's a cinch old sourpuss can't hold it any longer."

"No, I suppose not," Kathy murmured. "And yet his

145

hand is healing beautifully. Of course it's stiff, and will be for a long time, but there hasn't been any infection at all. Dr. Elliott is wonderful in cases like that. It is a liberal education to work with him."

"Waking up, aren't you?" her friend said. Then she added, "It's about time. Bill Elliott is one of the world's best, just as I've been telling you for lo, these many moons. I shouldn't say you were exactly dumb, Kathy," she went on. "Just slow on the uptake. But more about Elliott anon. Tell me, were there fireworks between Mac and the Chief? Somehow I can't see MacDonald toadying to the old war horse."

"He didn't," Kathy said, "and yet the Chief seemed to submit to his suggestions. Not in a friendly spirit, of course. In fact he was even harsher than ever, but he did what Dr. MacDonald told him to do. I wonder if all that talk of enmity between them wasn't largely gossip. After all, Irene, they are both surgeons—good ones, too."

"So what?" the older nurse muttered. "Being surgeons doesn't make them immune to the ordinary failings of the human race. However, the probabilities are that the Chief knew when he was licked."

"Maybe," Kathy agreed and changed the subject. The day was cool for June, with a breeze blowing from the south that, despite the chill, brought odors of lilacs and hidden violets. Kathy took a little skip of pure joy and caught Irene's hand, and they stopped to watch a robin tugging at a long piece of string that refused to come loose. Suddenly another bird joined in the attempt but without success, and at last, in apparent disgust, they gave it up and flew away.

"Quitters!" scoffed Irene. "You know, I think robins are very stupid. I have watched them on the lawn of the annex while an alley cat kept an acquisitive eye on them. They would dig away after worms, seeming oblivious of that cat, until I couldn't stand it any longer and took a hand. I drove both robins and their potential slayer off to other fields. And do you know what Bob Channing said when he saw me taking sides like that? He reminded me that I, too, liked chicken, so why not let a poor starved feline enjoy a like feast?"

"He had something there, Irene," Kathy murmured. "Here comes a bus. It isn't crowded, either." She hailed it with a lifted hand, and the two nurses climbed aboard to ride down to the center of the city.

"I'd much rather have walked," the older nurse said, as they got out in front of Madame Berthe's swank dress shop. But I knew we would have plenty of walking before we got through—that is, if things go according to rule. There, Kathy," she exclaimed, "there's you frock right there, that green one in the window. I can see you in it."

"H'mm, I don't know," the younger girl murmured. "I had almost made up my mind to get something blue. Something soft and rather plain, if you know what I mean. After all, it's not my party, and I have no desire to look conspicuous. And blue goes well with almost everything."

"So does green," Irene pointed out. "If you don't believe it, look around you. Green everywhere. It's the season for green, and it's your color. I vote for that dress, Kathy, but let's go inside and look over the entire stock. I feel a bit extravagant just now. I haven't been on a spending spree in ages."

Madame Berthe, a large, beautifully proportioned, and handsomely gowned woman with lovely white hair piled on her majestic head, came to meet them. They were, at the time, the sole customers, and she appeared glad to see them. She led them to a small room in the rear and rang for various frocks to be displayed, while the girls sat comfortably, enjoying the unusual attention.

Madame chose a slim black frock for Irene that sloughed pounds from her plump figure, and the girl could scarcely believe that her "on again, off again" diet hadn't accomplished the miracle after all.

"Black is always slimming," Kathy assured her, "and you look like a million in it. I'm sure it is your dress, Irene. I love it."

The older nurse had already chosen a plain tailored suit of gray sharkskin that required almost no alterations, and she was jubilant.

"Somehow finding something that is exactly right does things to one's ego, Kathy," she said, as she watched the parade of frocks displayed before them.

"Green is for you, mademoiselle," Madame Berthe assured the younger girl, bringing out a particularly beautiful creation and spreading it on the table before her. "If any of my girls were available, I am sure you would be convinced, but what with sickness, weddings, vacations, and such, I am at my wit's end. Won't you try this on?"

But Kathy shook her head. "It is much too elaborate for me—for this occasion, madame," she said, almost regretfully, for the gown was beautiful and she wanted it. "Green is all right, if I can find the frock I want. It isn't so much the color as the style—the model."

"I understand," the woman murmured and departed to return with another.

This time Kathy exclaimed, "There! That's my dress. If it fits, that is exactly what I had in mind."

It fitted as if made for her, and the girl was delighted, although Irene declared it was much too plain.

"Plain!" Madame scoffed. "But the workmanship! The style—the snap—the chic, if you please——"

"And," Kathy groaned, "the price!"

"Forget the price, darling," Irene told her, feeling that she, herself, had come off very well indeed. "It will last for ages. A dress like that is really an investment. You'll get a lot of good out of it."

Madame promised to have the purchases delivered before five that same evening, and they left, window shopping until they came to Bostwick's favorite Bonnet Shop, and here again they found themselves welcomed.

"What gives?" Irene murmured cautiously. "Is this a holiday of some kind? Where are all the customers?"

It was much easier here to find what they wanted, and both girls left with a feeling of accomplishment. Their shopping spree had turned out satisfactorily. Four o'clock. The afternoon had gone swiftly, and they were hungry.

"It's my treat," Irene declared, as they approached a fashionable midtown restaurant. "Let's go in here. I feel like having a good hearty tea, or even another lunch. I'd say dinner if it were a bit later, but let's have a really good lunch, Kathy."

"Why should it be your treat, Irene?" Kathy asked. "You've spent a lot of money, and I'm perfectly able to pay my own way and yours too, for that matter. O.K., O.K.!" she cried, at the other's glare of offended dignity. "Only——"

148

"Only nothing," Irene muttered, as they followed a waiter to a table in the well-filled room. "And don't spare the expense, remember. I'll probably get it out of you some other time. Let's eat well and enjoy it. It has been a good day, and I'm pleased with our purchases."

They spent an hour over that lunch and returned to the hospital just as dinner was being served, but neither girl wanted dinner and were eager to view what they had bought. Irene brought her packages across the hall, because she thought Kathy's mirror the more flattering. The hats were tried on first and disposed of, and then Irene modeled her new frock, which was so becoming that it brought forth oh's and ah's from an uninvited audience in the doorway. The suit didn't fare quite so well, but when Irene mentioned the price, the oh's became shrieks of dismay.

"Wait until you see Kathy in her new party dress," Irene told them, as she slipped out of the flattering black for the second time. "And wait until you hear what it set her back. But either come in or stay out. It may be June, but it's still mighty cool, and I'm only half clad, remember. Slip it on and knock 'em dead, darling," she urged, as three nurses in the doorway stepped into the room and closed the door. "You'll love her in it."

But the audience was disappointed in Kathy's new frock, as she felt sure they would be. It was much too plain for the average taste.

"No like?" Irene asked. "It cost a fortune—it has style, workmanship, snap, and chic. Don't show your ignorance. And don't pay any attention to them, Kathy," she went on. "It's marvelous on you, and I am willing to wager you'll be the hit of the evening. Beat it, you gate crashers!" she ordered and opened the door wide for their departure.

One of them turned as she reached the door to say, "You don't really mind our lack of enthusiasm, do you, Marshall? I guess we though it was a real party dress, not a—a dinner frock, perhaps. But on you it looks swell, anyway." The door closed behind her. Kathy laughed.

Both nurses changed quickly into uniform and hurried to their respective patients. Somehow Kathy had lost her fear of the Chief but wondered just how he would take being ousted or retired from his position as Chief of Staff. In a way she dreaded meeting him—the fallen god, the idol of so many former patients and surgeons alike—but even though no one really liked the man, there were many who recognized his ability and admired him accordingly.

But Dr. Blaine said not one word of the Board Meeting, and Kathy lacked the temerity to broach the subject. She would hear about it later, for she knew that Dr. Elliott had been present at that meeting, although she wondered why, because he was still only senior intern. Perhaps it was because of his success in treating the Chief. She didn't know, but felt sure he would tell her all about it later.

The meeting had been scheduled for three that afternoon, and Sam Bostwick was next to the last to arrive. He came alone. He had just taken his place at the end of the table in the long, somewhat luxurious Board room, when Dr. Blaine, entered, found a seat in an obscure corner, and responded to greetings with his usual stiff nod. His manner discouraged conversation, and inquiries as to his health were met with mere grunts. But since he had never been a friendly or demonstrative man, no one expected anything else from him. He was indeed a strange creature.

Sam Bostwick called the meeting to order. The usual procedure was followed—minutes read, further suggestions and comments on the proposed addition to the children's section made, applications of several medical students for internships in the hospital considered. Then came the question of a new Chief of Staff to replace Dr. Blaine, who had for so many years given of his time, his talents, and his strength to their beloved Bostwick Memorial Hospital.

An old lady stood up. "I move that we give Dr. Blaine a vote of thanks," she said quaveringly and sat down.

There was a quick seconding of the motion and a unanimous clapping of hands, but no change appeared in the grim face of the man who stared straight ahead, his eyes unblinking.

A man this time, elderly as were most of the others, rose to make the motion that Dr. Blaine be asked to remain as advising surgeon to his successor, whoever he might be. That, too, was quickly seconded and carried with accompanying applause. There was a pause here, and people became restless.

The chairman lifted a paper from the table before him and began to read a list of names of surgeons who might be interested in taking over the job of Chief of Staff. It was a long list. The first name mentioned was that of Dr. Scott, a man of integrity and skill only surpassed by their own Dr. Blaine. That idea was tabled to be considered later. Dr. Blaine remained silent. He had nothing to say for or against Dr. Scott nor, for that matter, about any others of the dozen or so names proposed. It was a splendid opportunity for any surgeon, and none of the Board members had any doubts of possible refusal of their offer, should one be made.

The meeting appeared to reach a deadlock. Sam Bostwick remained quite neutral. He advanced no name for the position, but left it entirely up to the meeting. Dr. Elliott fidgeted, and Miss Merriman, her eyes moist from unshed tears, sat by his side, wishing the Chief would say something. Dr. Elliott cast a sidelong glance at the man in the corner, who sat with bowed head, apparently quite unmoved by what was going on around him.

At last the Chairman of the Board said, almost regretfully, "We have given you a number of names—good men, all. Suppose we ask Dr. Blaine to make a suggestion, to give us an idea of which man he would want to succeed him as Chief of Staff here at Bostwick Memorial. After all, Dr. Blaine is familiar with most of the eminent surgeons in the country and should be in a far better position to name his successor than any of us here. Dr. Blaine?"

The Board members waited for the Chief to rise. It seemed almost as if it was too much to expect of him, but at last he got slowly to his feet. His hand and arm were still closely bandaged, scars were still apparent on his broad face, but his steely eyes and grim mouth were as uncompromising as ever.

"Mr. Chairman and members of the Board governing Bostwick Memorial Hospital," he began, and cleared his throat loudly. "I neither approve nor disapprove of any of the men suggested here this afternoon as my possible successor. That is, of course, up to the members of the Board. I have only this to say—and I say it after due

151

consideration." The frog in his throat seemed persistent. His voice deepened until it filled the whole room. "Why go afield when we have in our midst the best man obtainable?"

There was not a sound in the room as they waited for him to go on. Miss Merriman caught Dr. Elliott's hand and hung on. Dr. Elliott held his breath. The pause, while brief, seemed endless to the silent group.

Dr. Blaine sighed deeply. "I would suggest for the position as Chief of Staff of this hospital a young man Bostwick born and bred—one who is known to most of you and who has proved himself to the complete satisfaction of all who know him—Dr. Gary MacDonald!"

There was a breathless moment, in which a sob escaped the Superintendent of Nurses and in which Dr. Elliott uttered a fervent, but silent, "Grand old sport!" Then he left his seat to slip into the one nearest the speaker.

"Back to your room, Doctor!" he said, under cover of the round of applause. "I never admired you more. Come on. Let's beat it before they mob you."

And later, in his room, the ex-Chief of Staff sat in silence, denying admittance to everyone excepting Bill Elliott, who refused to be shut out.

CHAPTER EIGHTEEN

A BROWN AND GOLD orchid arrived at Kathy Marshall's room in the annex the next afternoon, Bill Elliott's card bearing the information that Irene had told him Kathy was to wear a green frock. He hoped she would like the orchid and that he would see her later.

"The man's psychic, Kathy!" Irene declared, as she admired the flower. "I never told him anything of the kind. In fact he didn't ask me. I merely mentioned that you and I had gone on a shopping spree and had managed to get exactly what we wanted."

"It doesn't matter," Kathy assured her, "only he need not have done it. Orchids cost plenty, and Bill is still just an intern."

"Oh, you!" cried the exasperated Irene. "Wear it and be thankful!"

"I intend to." Kathy smiled.

"Is he escorting you to the party?" Irene asked.

"Pete Adams is coming for me early. I just had a telephone call from Dana. Do you know, Irene?" she went on softly. "Dana is ecstatically happy. Isn't it wonderful?"

"Probably," her friend said. "But being the wife of a doctor or even a surgeon isn't all beer and skittles, don't make any mistakes about it."

Kathy laughed. "And yet you are planning on just that," she jeered.

"Oh, my case is different. Bob and I are past our first youth. We're mature, sensible. We know——"

"Oh, sure!" Kathy grinned. "Of course."

"This Pete Adams, Kathy," Irene asked after a moment, as she watched her friend's preparations for the evening. "Just how old is he? College, isn't he?"

Kathy felt the blood rush to her face and turned her back on the inquisitor. "Oh, Pete's somewhere around twenty or twenty-one, with two years more of college. He's a good youngster, and——"

"I bet a dollar he's in love with you," the other interrupted. "Dana wants you to marry him, doesn't she? Don't tell me a thing, Kathy. I believe I'm sort of psychic myself. Poor Bill!"

"Don't be silly!" Kathy said sharply. "Pete's only a boy. I'm years older—in experience. And don't waste any sympathy on Dr. Elliott. I'm sure he doesn't need it."

"Sorry," Irene murmured, and prepared to leave the room.

"Oh, Irene!" Kathy cried contritely. "Forgive me. I didn't mean to speak so crossly, but why can't people leave me alone? First Dana and now you."

"Then I was right!" Irene said triumphantly.

"Dana's in love," Kathy explained. "That's all she can think of. Well, how do I look? Oh, the orchid! I mustn't forget that. Pin it on for me, will you?"

"You look sweet, Kathy," the older nurse told her, "and at the risk of incurring your anger I'm going to give you a bit of advice. Don't let your fondness for Dana Adams and her family get you into trouble. I'll keep my fingers crossed and may even say a small prayer for you. 'By, darling," she said, as she laid Kathy's light evening wrap about her shoulders. "Have a grand time and give the happy couple my felicitations."

She went to the window and watched as Kathy left the building with Dana's tall young brother, who seemed unnecessarily attentive as he walked her to the waiting car. "H'm'm," she muttered to herself. "Bill Elliott had better do something more than send orchids if he wants Kathy Marshall. It looks to me as if that lad out there means business."

And at the spacious Hammond home Dr. Elliott was thinking much the same thing, for young Pete Adams seldom left Kathy's side. Kathy had heard something of the Board Meeting and of Gary MacDonald's appointment to the post of Chief of Staff of Memorial to replace Dr. Blaine. She wanted to get the details and hear everything that had happened, but Dr. Elliott appeared preoccupied with one of the other guests, and anyway Pete Adams was always there beside her. Then Dr. MacDonald took a hand.

"Dana told me you had heard the news, Marsh— Kathy," he said, coming to stand beside her. "It's a great responsibility, and I'm glad to know that you will be a member of the staff, for a while, at least. You and Dr. Elliott are an unbeatable pair. He has just been telling me about the Board Meeting. I know that it must have cost Dr. Blaine untold agony of spirit to relinquish his position —and to a younger man. Bill tells me he did it with unexpected graciousness. I am glad. Doctor!" he called. "Take Miss Marshall into the library and tell her what you told me about the Board Meeting.... Bill's a fine raconteur," he went on, and as they moved away, his arm on Pete's shoulder, Kathy heard him tell the young man that he hadn't had a chance to ask about college.

"I began to think that we should never get you away from Pete," Dr. Elliott murmured, as they left the room. He steered her not toward the library but outside, where a white path led to a summerhouse a short distance away.

"Will you be cold, Kathy?" he asked solicitously. "If you will promise not to vanish I'll slip back to the house and get you a wrap—O.K.," he added hastily, as Kathy shook her head, "we'll be inside anyway .... I discovered this place earlier in the evening and hoped to keep the knowledge to myself," he went on. "Did you like the orchid, Kathy?"

He touched it gently, and the girl smiled. "You're extravagant, Doctor," she chided, "but I love it. It's my second orchid."

"Your second? How about your first one? Someone special?"

"Oh, no, just a boy I knew back home."

"Are you happy about this engagement—I mean Mac and Dana's—Kathy?" he asked abruptly.

"Why, of course," she replied, her heart racing. What did he mean? Was he too laboring under the delusion that she loved Dr. MacDonald? "Why do you ask?"

"Someone, I don't recall who it was exactly, intimated some time ago that you and Mac might make a go of it, and I—well, it was a blow to me because from the very first I wanted you for myself. Do you mind?"

"Mind?" Kathy asked, quite unaware that she had spoken.

"Yes," he said. "Of course you know I am in love with you—everyone else does—and I hope you will consent to become my wife. My uncle, who happens to be a physician, is urging me to take over his practice. He says he wants to retire, but you and I know that doctors never retire. They die in harness, and Uncle Fred will too, but he wants me to come in with him and take over. He says he's tired, wants to go fishing. He has a big practice. It's in a small town, to be sure, but among fine people, and he is sure I shall be a success. Dr. MacDonald wants me to remain here, even if I take on an independent practice. He says he wants to be able to call on me when he needs me. What do you think, Kathy? Does living in a small Wisconsin town appeal to you?"

"Wisconsin!" cried Kathy. "Why, my people live in Wisconsin! It would be like going home——" She paused.

The young man was quick to say, "Then you will come with me—to Wisconsin? Darling, darling, I love you so very much!"

"I—I don't know, Bill," the girl demurred, drawing back from his encircling arms. "I like you, but—I'm not sure about loving you, and I must be sure. It wouldn't be fair to either of us, you know, if——"

"Give me a chance, Kathy," Bill Elliott pleaded. "I haven't much to offer you right now, I know—compared to Gary MacDonald——"

"There is no comparison, Bill," Kathy said quickly,

155

'and if you are willing to wait, to give me time to be sure——"

This time the eager arms would not be denied, and Kathy didn't resist but lifted her face for his kiss.

It was upon this scene, clearly visible in the moonlight, that Peter Adams, searching for the missing Kathy, came suddenly. Strangely he was not too surprised. Somehow he had suspected something of the sort. He attempted to withdraw quietly, but in retreating he knocked against a tall urn, which promptly toppled over with a loud thump. Peter fled, and the two inside the summerhouse drew apart.

Butch called from the kitchen porch, "Last call to dinner! Loiterers continue doing so at their own risk. Hurry up, you star gazers, I'm hungry!" He caught his brother's arm and demanded what ailed him, anyway.

"Leave me alone, Butch," Peter replied shortly. "This should be a wholesale announcement party. I'm getting out!"

"Gosh, Pete!" Butch remonstrated. "You can't. Gram won't like it, and anyway I always knew Doc Elliott had the inside track there. You must have, too, though I can't see what she sees in that old pill-pusher. Why, he must be as old as Gary, or almost as old. What ails gals nowadays?"

"Oh, go roll your hoop!" was Peter's ungracious retort, as he pulled away from his brother's restraining arm and disappeared into the house.

And out in the garden the culprits walked with leisurely tread back to the house, through the side porch, and into the library, to be greeted by the prospective bride and groom with demands as to where they had been all evening.

"All evening!" cried Dr. Elliott indignantly. "We weren't gone more than a few minutes. What do you mean, all evening?"

"Well, you're here at last, and Gram and Mrs. Mac-Donald are slowly going mad for fear dinner will be spoiled. You—you look different, somehow," Dana said, examining the two before them. "Don't you think so, Gary?"

Dr. MacDonald laughed. "They look as if certain difficulties and uncertainties have been ironed out satisfactorily. Why not make it a double announcement? O.K.?"

"Of course not," Kathy said quickly.

"That's up to Kathy's family, Doctor," Bill Elliott added.

"Better wipe off the lipstick, Bill," Gary advised.

"No, don't," Dana pleaded. "Leave it on, and there will be no need of an announcement. You're lovely when you blush, Kathy," she told her friend, hugging her happily. "But," she whispered, "poor Pete!"

Butch appeared in the open door and murmured aggrievedly, "I don't care much for announcement parties. Everyone involved appears to be nuts. If being in love does that to people, preserve me! I'm hungry!"

"Poor Butch!" his sister crooned, slipping one arm through his and the other through that of her fiancé. "Let's lead the way. We'll wait right here until the others fall in line. You're to sit next to us, you two," she told Kathy and Bill Elliott. "I guess Gary's psychic, aren't you, dear?" Dr. MacDonald nodded and grinned at his friend.

"Is it all off?" Dr. Elliott asked, scrubbing his mouth with his once immaculate handkerchief.

"Almost," Kathy answered, pink-cheeked, and did a bit of scrubbing on the chin so near her own. Her eyes were dark with excitement, and he caught her hand and leaned closer but she drew back. "Not here, Bill," she warned, and the couple ahead turned to repeat her warning.

The procession moved slowly toward the dining room, and the remainder of the evening passed according to schedule. If anyone noticed the absence of Peter Adams, nothing was said; only Gram, from time to time, cast an anxious eye about the room. Somehow she sensed the turn of events, even though she said nothing, for after dinner Butch disappeared too, and she hoped the boys were together.

It wasn't until Dr. Elliott's car stopped before the annex sometime later that Kathy heard the young man's report on the Board Meeting. But even that seemed to have lost its importance. Kathy was already looking ahead to the time when she would be back in her own beloved Wisconsin, able to run in on her family whenever the longing became almost unbearable. She smiled to herself. Why, she was actually acting as if it were all settled—as if Bill and she were really engaged—as if she were sure she loved him. Suddenly she knew that she did.

"We will have a good life, darling," the young man whispered as Kathy prepared to leave the car. "I have felt from the first that we were meant for each other. You'll like Uncle Fred. He's a grand old chap, a widower for years. His housekeeper, Polly Gibson, was his and later Aunt Maggie's nurse—practical, of course, but a sweet old soul. Of course we need not live there if you don't want to——"

Kathy laughed somewhat hysterically. "You're a fast worker, Bill," she chided. "We're not even engaged yet."

"Might as well be, darling," he told her. "Three people at the party reminded me of lipstick, so I guess we didn't get it all off. Yours must be the sort that stays on and on and on, as the ads promise. But inasmuch as it is yours, I don't mind." He walked her to the front door of the annex where Irene Barker was waiting.

She opened the door and greeted the latecomers. "I was just about to retire for the night—or what's left of it. Do you realize what time it is? But don't look. Good night, Doctor," she said pointedly. "I read somewhere that partings should be brief."

"Better practice what you preach, Barker," the young man jeered, as he went down the walk to the curb where his car was parked. "I could tell tales if I wanted to. But thanks for waiting up, pal!"

"So!" Irene said, as she slipped an arm through that of her friend and accompanied her up the three flights of stairs. "You have at last come to your senses. Good for you! The atmosphere of the place— or was it the occasion? All settled?"

"I suppose so," Kathy murmured dubiously. "And yet—oh, I don't know, Irene," she added, for now that she was back in the hospital she was again uncertain.

"You're tired, darling," her friend comforted. "Try to sleep, though I bet you won't—not much, anyway. Still, you have tomorrow off until three and should be able to get some rest. But let me tell you something, Kathy Marshall. It's a big relief to me—and from this time

158

forward I'm a firm believer in prayer." She kissed Kathy softly and turned to leave the room.

And as she knelt before her bed that night, Kathy Marshall prayed for guidance and then thanked God for the love of so fine a man as Bill Elliott.

Although she had expected to remain awake until morning, she was surprised to find the sun shining brightly when at last she opened her eyes. She lay and stretched for a moment, wondering at the feeling of well-being that flooded her heart. There came a soft knock on her door, and at her reply the maid entered with a long box—unmistakably flowers. Kathy blushed, as she took it, and thanked the girl. She held the box for a long moment before she opened it. Long-stemmed roses—quantities of them! She buried her face in their fragrant beauty and shyly reached for the card that accompanied them, although she knew who had sent them.

Kathy:
Just to remind you of last night, my darling, and to repeat that I love you with all my heart. The new boss is giving us both the afternoon and evening off duty. I'll see you at two, Kathy. Until then, all my love until death and after.

Bill

Kathy sighed deeply. So it was all settled, at least as far as Bill was concerned. She cradled the roses close to her heart and breathed their heady perfume. Dear Bill! Dear, dependable Bill! So this was love—this serenity, this sweet contentment, this eagerness to share whatever life might hold in store if Bill was with her, this facing the future with confidence, knowing that whatever happened Bill would be there . . . .

Another knock on the door came, and this time it was Irene Barker.

"I bring you felicitations, darling," she said, stooping to kiss the flushed face on the pillow. "I hoped to be the first today, but I find someone has beat me to it. No need to ask. So you are to have a holiday? Lucky you! And now no more hospital uniforms for you, honey child. Already your life pattern has changed. Another evening free from the eternal grind. Lucky, lucky you!"

159

"How did you know?" Kathy asked, releasing the flowers to her friend.

"Oh, I told you I was psychic," Irene answered. "One has only to catch a fleeting glimpse of Dr. Elliott to know he has won the jackpot. I even congratulated him, and I thought he was going to kiss me. But he evidently thought better of it—darn it!"

Kathy laughed and swung her feet out of bed and into her slippers. "I slept like a baby last night, Irene," she said, almost apologetically. "I shouldn't have, should I? What does that prove?"

"That you were about worn out, stupid," her friend answered. "But I'm willing to bet a dollar that Elliott didn't sleep. The guy looked dopey, and I suggested that he sneak off and get some shut-eye, but he assured me that he was far too busy — that sleep was the furthest thing from his thoughts at present. Gosh, Kathy!" she said whimsically. "To think you are capable of doing such things to a man like Bill Elliott! It's certainly amazing what love will do. Better get dressed if you want any lunch."

They went downstairs together, and Kathy felt sure the nurses in the dining room must be fully aware of conditions, for they nodded and smiled and, when they passed her chair, whispered wishes of good will. It was all heartening, and gradually the strangeness of it all disappeared. When she left the room after a scanty lunch Kathy knew that she was committed for all time and felt a deep and abiding happiness. Yes, this was love. She knew it now and was glad.

THE END